# The Rats of Montsouris

Léo Malet was born in Montpellier in 1909. He had no formal education and began as a cabaret singer at 'La vache enragée' in Montmarte in 1925. He became an anarchist and contributed to various magazines: *L'Insurgé, Journal de l'Homme aux sandales* . . . He had various jobs: office worker, ghost writer, manager of a fashion magazine, cinema extra, newspaper seller . . .

From 1930 to 1940 he belonged to the Surrealist Group and was a close friend of André Breton, René Magritte and Yves Tanguy. During that time he published several collections of poetry.

In 1943, inspired by the American writers Raymond Chandler and Dashiel Hammett, he created Nestor Burma, the Parisian private detective whose first mystery *120, rue de la Gare* was an instant success and marked the beginning of a new era in French detective fiction.

More than sixty novels were to follow over the next twenty years. Léo Malet won the 'Grand Prix de la Littérature policière' in 1947 and the 'Grand Prix de l'humour noir' in 1958 for his series 'Les nouveaux mystères de Paris', each of which is set in a different *arrondissement*. *The Rats of Montsouris*, depicting the 14th *arrondissement*, was first published in 1955.

Lés Malet lives in Châtillon, just south of Paris.

G000245935

Also by Léo Malet in Pan Books

120 rue de la Gare

Léo Malet

# *The Rats of Montsouris*

translated from the French by Peter Hudson
general editor: Barbara Bray

Pan Books
London, Sydney and Auckland

First published in France 1955 by
Robert Laffont, Paris

Published in France 1982 by Editions Fleuve Noir
as *Les Rats de Montsouris*

This edition first published in Great Britain 1991 by
Pan Books Ltd, Cavaye Place, London SW10 9PG

9 8 7 6 5 4 3 2 1

© Léo Malet 1955

This English translation © Aramos 1991

ISBN 0 330 31847 0

Photypeset by Input Typesetting Ltd, London
Printed in England by Clays Ltd, St Ives plc

*to Paulette*

in memory of the 14th Arrondissement
and all that goes with it

# Contents

1 Louvre
2 Bourse
3 Temple
4 Hôtel-de-Ville
5 Panthéon
6 Luxembourg
7 Palais-Bourbon
8 Elysée
9 Opéra
10 Entrepôt
11 Popincourt
12 Reuilly
13 Gobelins
14 Observatoire
15 Grenelle/Vaugirard
16 Passy/Auteuil
17 Batignolles-Monceau
18 Butte-Montmartre

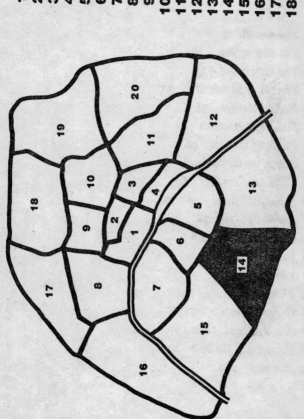

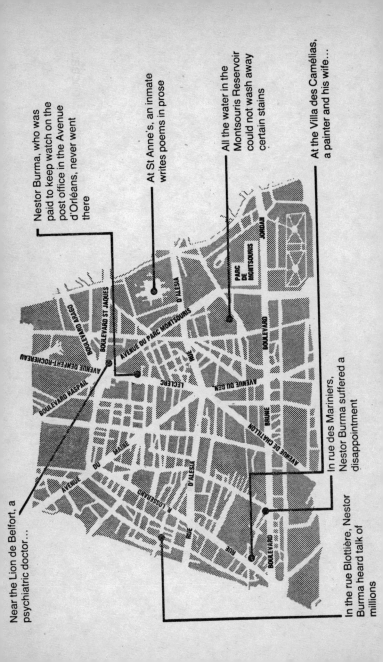

Near the Lion de Belfort, a psychiatric doctor…

Nestor Burma, who was paid to keep watch on the post office in the Avenue d'Orléans, never went there

At St Anne's, an inmate writes poems in prose

All the water in the Montsouris Reservoir could not wash away certain stains

At the Villa des Camélias, a painter and his wife…

In rue des Mariniers, Nestor Burma suffered a disappointment

In the rue Blottière, Nestor Burma heard talk of millions

# 1 *The weasel*

It was one of those summer nights we don't get often enough. Just the way I like them: dry and stifling, without the hint of a breeze, not even the prospect of a deceptively refreshing storm. Baking hot; or boiling, according to taste. Barometers were going mad; the thinnest possible sheet must have weighed a ton.

The rue du Cange was damp and torpid. Scorchers usually stimulate conversation, but not tonight. Even in this crowded district there wasn't a single concierge holding court on her doorstep.

Through the open windows of a seedy hotel you could hear the poor devils inside tossing and turning in their unlit rooms, the bedsprings grating as they struggled in vain against the bedbugs. A train from the Gare de Montparnasse, struggling through the heavy night air, clattered across some nearby points.

No other sound disturbed the clammy quiet. The noise of the train grew faint, then died on a brief and distant hoot, bearing a load of blissful holiday-makers to Brittany and sea breezes. Near to where I was, a drain gave off a fetid stench from the sewers.

I came out into the rue du Moulin-de-la-Vierge.

But there were neither windmills nor virgins at the intersection with the rue de l'Ouest. Only a swarthy little fellow who must have been from somewhere in the East. He was coming out of the bar I was about to go into on what I suppose you could call business. He slid away furtively into the darkness in the direction of the rue Raymond-Losserand, which used to be the rue de Vanves.

Inside the dimly lit bar there reigned the same oppressive calm as in the streets. It was like one of those English clubs I've heard about, where silence is compulsory, only this wasn't so clean and there weren't so many people.

The low ceiling had seen as much tobacco as the inside of my pipe, and the posters on the walls were so fly-blown you couldn't read the words.

Behind a battered zinc counter covered with circular winestains a flabby-looking heavyweight in a vest, evidently the manager of the establishment, was washing glasses in dish-water seasoned with the sweat pouring from his face and arms. He didn't look happy.

On the paying side of the counter there was just one customer. As inelegantly dressed as I was, he was warily examining a glass of doubtful-looking wine, though it was certainly not his first. When I came in he merely glanced at me, then went back to his drink. Neither he nor the giant in the vest answered my gentlemanly 'Good evening'. It was too hot to be wasting words. Shut your mouth and keep it shut was the order of the night.

The only sound, apart from the swilling of dish-water, came from the back room, separated off by a swing door, where billiard balls could be heard knocking against each other. Nothing else. The players didn't feel the need for comment.

I leaned my elbow on the counter. The boss abandoned his washing-up and surprised me by opening his mouth on some rather grey teeth.

'What'll it be?' he said.

'A beer.'

'Large or small?'

'Small,' I said.

He sighed, took a squat bottle from the ice-box, removed the top with a deft flick of the wrist, grabbed one of the glasses set out to dry, and banged it and the bottle down in front of me. Then he sighed again and went back to his washing up, morose as ever. His hundred kilos were feeling the 28 degrees shown on the Cinzano thermometer.

I poured out my beer and drank half of it straight off. It wasn't sensational, but it was cool and went down nicely. I expected someone to give an opinion on the heat wave, but none was forthcoming. The ivory went on cannoning on the tables next door. I got out my pipe, took my time filling and lighting it, asked the manager where the 'gents' was, and in the same leisurely fashion went through into the back room.

It was a fair size, but without windows or any other doors. The two billiard tables were quite a luxury for a dump like that. Both were occupied, one by a pair of workmen and the other by a lone player practising difficult shots. The only light came from lamps hanging over the tables. The players moved like shadows round the pools of light, while inside the glare the balls swirled as sleekly and coyly as fashionable ladies at the races.

I watched the players at the first table for a moment, then made my way towards the man playing solo. He was tall and angular, afflicted with a nose like an ice-pick between prominent cheek-bones à la Simone Signoret. But the resemblance stopped there: a thatch of black hair crowned all. Forty years old, and not a tooth of his own in his head, if my memory served. (He'd had them pulled out one by one so as to be rejected for active service.)

His light-coloured jacket lay on a chair, and he'd rolled up the sleeves of a white shirt that owed nothing to Persil. A tattoo mark inside his right forearm depicted an anchor with an extremely poisonous-looking snake twined round it. Its colours were faded. He must have tried to have it removed, but you'd need to be blind not to notice it, especially as he now made no effort to hide it. Perhaps he'd changed his mind.

He sprawled out over the green baize, preparing one of the master shots the experts discuss at such length. His right arm lay directly under the light, as though he wanted me to admire the mess he'd made of it. Finally he straightened up a bit, attempted a cannon . . . and bungled it.

I couldn't help letting out a muffled exclamation. He stood up so that his head was in the shadow.

'No much cop, eh?' he said. He had a hoarse, low voice like someone with a throat problem. Or with good reason for not being clearly heard.

'I'm not a connoisseur,' I said. 'And maybe I put you off.'

He didn't answer. He'd begun to chalk his cue in expert fashion with a blue cube held in the palm of his hand. The players at the next table went on with their game, regardless. I played the inveterate gasbag.

'It's like the horses,' I said. 'All right so long as you stick to theory, but as soon as you put any money down everything goes to blazes. Except the nags, of course. They never get beyond the starting post.'

I knocked my pipe out on my worn-down heel.

'It only takes some idiot to come and start watching you,' I said, 'and you miss your shot.'

The man with the tattoo reacted briefly but eloquently to my interference.

'Yeah.'

'Sorry if I bothered you,' I added, clinging like a conscientious leech.

'It doesn't matter.'

He dropped his chalk and began to stare at the bull's

head carved on my pipe. I slowly filled it again, letting the light fall full on me.

'Interested in my pipe, are you? Nice, isn't it? Everyone admires it.'

So far he'd been chilly despite the heat wave, but now he seemed to thaw.

'Is it the only one like it?' he asked.

'You're not going to tell me you want it, are you?' I said. 'What makes you ask?'

'Er . . . I knew someone once . . .'

He stopped and came round the table to get a better look at me, then let out a long chuckle.

'Good God!' he said, his porcelain teeth gleaming between his thin lips. 'I think you're the person I'm talking about.'

'Who was that?' I said. 'My name's Saubert.'

'Saubert. That's right.'

I put my head on one side to study his face more closely. People always do that, I've never understood why. But one has to stick to tradition.

'Yes, yes, yes,' I said, on various different notes. 'I've got it now. Stalag XB, wasn't it?'

'That's right. My name's Ferrand.'

'Of course!' I said, pretending to be surprised. 'Ferrand! It's a small world.'

'Very small,' he said in a strange voice.

We shook hands.

'What've you been up to?' I asked.

He shrugged.

'This and that.'

'I'm at a loose end,' I sighed. 'Down and out, actually. I hang around this area because there's a branch of the Salvation Army not far away. I came to see if I could scrounge a meal, but it's shut. Never mind. Tomorrow is another day. As for getting somewhere to sleep, I can manage out of doors – it's not snowing.'

I stopped to draw breath, and stared at my ex-fellow-prisoner's hatchet face as if it was the most interesting thing I'd ever seen.

'Ferrand! Well, well, well! What a stroke of luck, running into an old mate like you! Er . . . The fact of the matter is. . . . You wouldn't have two or three hundred francs to spare by any chance, would you? In memory of the barbed wire, and without letting the Maréchal know, as we used to say! Just to give my bull his ration of grass? After that I'll manage.'

He'd been expecting as much. He took two filthy hundred-franc notes out of his trouser pocket and held them out. I put them into mine with a grateful smile.

'How about buying you a drink as interest on the loan?'

He pulled a face.

'No thanks,' he said in a voice as dry as the night outside, despite the amount he'd certainly put away.

But I insisted, and finally he accepted just to get rid of me.

We went back and sat in the bar. The lone drinker had disappeared, but the boss was still trying to beat the heat by sluicing his glassware. We interrupted his ablutions by ordering a Vichy water and a beer.

Ferrand (as in Clermont-Ferrand) didn't seem overcome with joy at having met a fellow ex-POW. He was unmoved by my memories of the more colourful events of our sojourn in Sandbostel (Hanover). He occasionally said 'Yeah!' or 'Right!', but didn't commit himself any further. He was merely tolerating me, if the way he rolled his eyes at the landlord was anything to go by. So, message received and understood, as they say in the so-called navy. And to think some people go to the cinema for entertainment!

I didn't want to outstay my welcome, so I paid for the

drinks, shook Ferrand by the hand and beat it. As I went out into the oven of the street I heard him say:

'Just another bum.'

'They're all the same,' the landlord answered slowly.

Now I understood why he was so silent. He only spoke when he had something original to say.

I made my way slowly to the rue Vercingétorix and began to wander down it, from the passage de Gergovie to the rue d'Alésia. I wasn't likely to attract too much attention. The street was as dead as the Gallic chieftain whose name it bears. Not a sound. It was like that sometimes in that area; ideal for meditation. Or for mugging. The street lamps might have been lighting up a graveyard. Two or three cars hurtled down the road, tearing up the melted tarmac, but their brief growl died almost as soon as it began, like certain love affairs.

At one point it looked as if the wilderness was about to come to life. A man with bandy legs turned into the street; but he soon went back the way he'd come. He must have been lost. With pins like that he was probably heading for Maisons-Lafitte and the races. Or maybe I'd scared him. It can happen. And the next night-bird seemed to confirm this theory. He was a civil-service type, probably tottering home after an evening out with friends. He gave me a strange look as we passed, one eye on me and the other looking round for the nearest telephone box to call the police. Then without more ado he plunged into a block of flats. The door slammed behind him, and a moment later a light came on higher up, so I knew that despite his haste he hadn't come to grief on the stairs. Then the light went out and the street was deserted once more.

The flats were no doubt full of people with their ears pricked up like owls, who wouldn't venture out even if a bomb went off, and who'd calculate the pros and cons if they heard someone being choked within an inch of his life. A quiet little spot ideal for dirty work in the small hours, all unsuspected by citizens who work all day and sleep all night. Such places look innocent enough in broad daylight, but in the dark they're unfriendly and disturbing. Especially if you have a dubious engagement. I hadn't bothered to bring a gun along, but I almost regretted it now.

I backed into a doorway to avoid being taken by surprise, and waited.

And for want of anything better to do I thought over all that had happened since that morning.

## 2  The man of law

It might have been about ten o'clock. Hélène and I were in the office, slaking our thirst. Sounds of the cheerful bustle in the rue des Petits-Champs drifted up through the open windows. The day promised to be hot, and it kept its word. The thermometer must already be at a giddy height. Paris hadn't had a summer like this since 1940. Habitual killjoys were beginning to wonder if it was a bad omen.

I'd taken off my jacket and tie, undone the top button of my shirt, and, both despite and because of the heat, lit my pipe. I sat blowing clouds of smoke towards the fan and watching them being cut to ribbons by the blades. I also examined my secretary as she sat at her desk.

They're all the same, I thought. They never have the courage of their convictions. Never carry things to their logical conclusion.

She was wearing a smart, light, brightly patterned dress, sleeveless and with a nice low neckline. It was the latter that was bothering me. You couldn't help but see into it, but you immediately came up against a brassière. Which in this temperature was both inappropriate and perverse. I was just about to tell her so when the phone rang.

'Hallo.'

'Hallo. Is that Nestor Burma?' came a stifled voice.

'Speaking.'

'This is Ferrand.'

The name didn't mean anything to me for a moment.

'Ferrand?'

'Paul Ferrand. We were prisoners of war together, and then—'

'Of course. I remember you now. Out of the nick, are you?'

'That's just it. I must see you.'

'All right,' I said. 'I'll leave a thousand francs with my concierge. Pick it up whenever you like.'

'You don't understand. I don't give a damn about your thousand francs. I'm not ringing just to touch you, even if I am broke. I have to see you.'

'Come over here, then.'

'No, I don't want to come to your place. Listen, this is how we'll arrange it . . .'

He explained the act he wanted me to put on, and I was so surprised I didn't offer any objection. So when he ended up with 'See you tonight, then,' I just said 'Right.'

'Who was that?' asked Hélène.

'Someone called Ferrand,' I said. 'He's a crook I met in POW camp. I've run into him occasionally since. He says he's just out of prison, which reminds me that the last I heard of him he was just going in for five years. I don't remember what for. But he's not a bad fellow – above the common run. Quite unusual, in fact. He wants to see me.'

'Nothing so extraordinary about that,' said Hélène.

'Wait till you hear,' I said. 'It's supposed to happen tonight in the 14th arrondissement – rue du Moulin-de-la-Vierge. I've got to dress up like a tramp and meet him as if by accident by a billiard table. And to make sure neither of us gets the wrong chap, I've got to smoke my bull's-head pipe and he's going to show me a tattoo mark. He can't know about the noble profession I exercise now. He must imagine I'm a film actor or something. All these penal reforms you hear about – they must have thrillers in the library at Fresnes nowadays, and Ferrand has read so many it's addled his brains.'

'Will you go?'

I laughed.

'Of course. Please note it down carefully if any other loonies ring up and want me to get myself up as a woman and stroll through the Bois, or wander along the canal Saint-Martin disguised as a priest, or undress altogether and stand in the Place de la Concorde stark naked. Anything to oblige.'

It was a little after three in the afternoon when I stopped the car in the place Jules-Hénaffe. I did have a car now. Nothing special. A reliable Dugat 12 with a boot big enough to stuff a couple of corpses in, if necessary: I've got a special knack for finding them. Just a piece of professional equipment, not flashy enough to give my clients the wrong idea. To be on the safe side, when I went to see them I parked it some distance away.

The little square was parched and brown, no rival for the nearby Parc Montsouris. The sun blazed down on the Montsouris Reservoir, which supplies part of the city with drinking water, and on its steep grass banks overlooking the avenue Reille. The building itself had a military air with its jaunty tiled belvedere; the year 1888 was inscribed on the cornice, as if the liquid it guarded were some vintage wine. Thick panes of frosted glass glinted in the sunshine. Fifty feet above me, a tallish man in a white coat was walking along the covered way round the reservoir as I progressed along the avenue Reille. Then he disappeared into a small structure that must have been the entrance to the damp underground corridors.

I walked along by the park for a while, then went up the rue Nansouty towards the boulevard Jourdan and the Cité Universitaire. My business lay in the rue du Douanier (not Rousseau), at a villa that stood out among all the other houses in the neighbourhood: modern mansions with huge bay windows, or more modest one-storey dwellings set in leafy seclusion and inhabited either by artists or people with plenty of money.

*The one I was going to must have dated from the beginning of the century. Its main floor was built well above ground level, and it was flanked on the left by what looked like a purely ornamental pepper-pot tower. A window box graced the sill of one of the tall, broad windows, and there were more flowers in the little front garden. Further back and partly hidden by a tree stood a stone figure of a woman, naked of course, and apparently trying to bathe her feet in a minute pool fed by a tiny fountain.*

*A dim-looking housemaid came to the door when I rang, her cheeks still red from the winds of her native heath.*

*'Is this M. Gaudebert's house, please?' I said.*

*'Yes, monsieur.'*

*'I have an appointment with him at half-past three. Here's my card.'*

*'Yes, monsieur. If monsieur would care to come this way.'*

*She showed me into a tastefully furnished sitting room and went off to tell her master I'd arrived. I was examining one of the numerous pictures on the walls when I heard a faint rustle, like that of a curtain falling back into place. I turned round expecting to see either the maid again or my potential client, but instead found standing before me a beautiful young woman.*

*She was twenty or so. Let's put it at twenty-three and leave it at that. Quite tall, with lovely though perhaps not naturally auburn hair. She'd had it cut short, which I thought a pity. Her eyes were almond shaped, or at least made up to look so, and golden brown in colour, with a strange light in them and faint shadows underneath which made her pure oval face even more interesting, if that were possible. Her nose was slender and sensuous; her mouth a graceful arc. She was wearing a grey pleated skirt and a revealing almost sleeveless low-necked jumper whose whiteness emphasized her tan.*

*She didn't say anything. Just stood looking at me inquiringly. I bowed.*

*'Good afternoon, mademoiselle,' I said. 'My name's Nestor*

*Burma. M. Gaudebert is expecting me. He called me at my office this morning.'*

*She ran the tip of her pink tongue over her lips and gave me a smile as soft as a caress.*

*'Yes, of course,' she said in a voice to match. 'I'm delighted to meet you, M. Nestor Burma.'*

*She took a step towards me and held out a hand as cool as morning dew. I noticed she wore nail varnish on her slender fingers.*

*At that moment the maid returned.*

*'Oh! Excuse me, madame,' she said.*

*Now I had addressed the young woman as 'mademoiselle', and she hadn't corrected me. I glanced at her hands. She was wearing several rings, but if there was a wedding ring among them I couldn't see it.*

*'M. Gaudebert will see you at once, monsieur,' said the maid.*

*I followed her out, bowing again as I did so. As we went up the stairs I asked:*

*'Is that the mistress of the house?'*

*'Yes, monsieur.'*

*I made no comment. My client was waiting at the top of the stairs.*

*He was a tall, thick-set man of about sixty, imposing despite being slightly overweight. His features were heavy; the right side of his mouth was twisted in a permanent grimace. He was losing his hair, but a pair of bushy eyebrows surmounted his unpleasantly cold and piercing eyes. He had plump white hands like an archbishop, but less than immaculate nails. In his striped trousers and black shoes he looked as if he was about to preside over a prize-giving, though he also wore a grey alpaca smoking jacket.*

*He led me into a study overlooking the Parc Montsouris, and as soon as we'd sat down he spoke.*

*'I've never heard anything but good of you, M. Nestor*

*Burma. And in the past our paths might easily have crossed professionally. But some time ago I decided to retire.'*

I said nothing.

'*I see my name doesn't mean anything to you. Never mind. I can ask what I have to ask without telling you my life story. All you need to know is that I'm being blackmailed and would like you to sort it out. I know who's responsible. He's a scoundrel. I should never have taken him in and let myself feel sorry for him.'*

He gave a short laugh.

'*Not like me at all! I suppose we change as we get older . . . Anyhow, I could go to the police, but . . .'*

'*But you won't.'*

'*Don't misunderstand me,'* he said curtly. '*I'm not afraid of them. It's just that they're too involved with the Law Courts. I'm well known there, and I don't want someone to speak out of turn and cause a scandal.'*

Something stirred in my unconscious when he mentioned the Law Courts.

'*No,'* he went on. '*I won't have any scandal, no matter where it comes from. That's what I'd like you to make this blackmailer understand. It would be too undignified for me to approach him myself. But you can tell him that if he persists I still have the power to break him to pieces. I hope he gets the message. Then you'll be the only person who knows anything about it. If he doesn't, I'll ask some old friends of mine to step in. I'd be sorry about that, but not nearly so sorry as he would.'*

'*Old friends . . . in the Law Courts?'*

Another brief laugh.

'*I think you're beginning to place me.'*

He'd slumped down in his chair, and his voice and expression had lost their sharpness.

'*I'm not the man I used to be. They put me in prison after the Liberation. Not for long, but it changed my outlook . . . Still, what's done is done. I have no regrets.'*

*I* suddenly snapped my fingers. Of course I knew who he was! He seemed to have gone to seed a bit, but perhaps that was the heat.

'Monsieur Armand Gaudebert!' I said. 'The famous public prosecutor!'

He drew himself up in his chair again, as cold and as stiff as the justice he'd so pitilessly served.

'Yes, monsieur,' he said. 'The same.'

A shiver ran down my spine. The study where we sat, the trees in the Parc Montsouris outside the window, everything was suddenly gone. It was as if I were the accused standing in the dock, a guard on either side of me, and before me all the ghouls who make up the audience at the Law Courts.

The public prosecutor who couldn't sleep if his victim's head failed to roll! (Not that that happened often!) The monster foreshadowed in the famous Willette cartoon of 1903, where a judge is shown throwing a decapitated head on to the dinner table and saying to his wife and children: 'Sorry I'm late, but here it is!'

So he'd had a taste of jug himself, and now he was being blackmailed. Once I got over the surprise it struck me as rather amusing. There was some justice after all. He should have been the last to complain. My reaction didn't escape him. He still had his old eagle eye.

'I wonder if we can still do business, M. Burma. This revelation has put you off, unless I'm much mistaken.'

'You are much mistaken,' I said. 'There have to be public prosecutors, I suppose. As far as I'm concerned you're just another client.'

'And now that I'm harmless and—'

'And have served your time – yes, I know. Let's get back to serious business. Who's trying to blackmail you, and why?'

'I've no idea why. Some extortionists put out feelers at random, thinking private individuals will react as certain banks do. I expect you know what I mean.'

'Yes. Some big banks which have absolutely nothing to hide pay up regularly just to avoid scandal. Some blackmailers make their living that way.'

'Precisely. So I don't know why. But I do know who. I have his name. And his address, more or less.'

'One of your former . . . ?' I said. 'No. How stupid of me. None of them would have a good enough . . . head on his shoulders to organize this kind of crime.'

'But he has got a record. Look at this.'

He took a sheet of paper from his blotter and held it out.

'It came this morning. His name's Ferrand.'

I couldn't help starting, but I said nothing. The message was made up of sentences and bits of sentences cut from a newspaper. It read:

'SEND 250,000 FRANCS IN USED 1000 FRANC NOTES MIXED SERIAL NUMBERS TO FERRAND POSTE RESTANTE CENTRAL POST OFFICE 14–15 AVENUE GENERAL LECLERC BY TOMORROW OTHERWISE STEPS WILL BE TAKEN.'

I handed the paper back.

'So, am I right in thinking you're going to send a parcel of paper cut to the appropriate size, and you want me to watch the counter, nab the fellow who picks it up and give him a message?'

'Exactly. Make him understand he'd better not go any further. Can you do that?'

'I can try. I'll have a chat with him. Old lags are always fond of a chinwag.'

A few minutes later we parted company on the best of terms, after Gaudebert had given me a suitable advance. And that's why I kept my appointment with Ferrand. And why, later the same night, I was leaning in a doorway, waiting.

# 3 The lady in red

A good half-hour after Ferrand and I had separated in a way that would have given idle observers the impression that he at least had no desire to renew our acquaintance, he arrived.

'Well?' I said.

'Decent of you to trust me,' he said quietly.

I'd been watching him as he came towards me on the other side of the street. He'd kept looking behind him as if he was afraid of being followed. Now he was rubbing his hands together, nervously rather than at the pleasure of seeing me again. As a result his jacket, draped over one shoulder like a toreador's cape, kept threatening to fall off, and he kept having to adjust it. He looked as if he had St Vitus's dance.

'It was something to do,' I said. 'I've got a bit of spare time at the moment and I haven't worn fancy dress for a long time.'

He looked me up and down, then gave a smile that was more like a grimace.

'You're just right for the part,' he said. 'And you carry it off a treat. You ought to go on the stage.'

'You too. As a director.'

His smile broadened a fraction.

'This must all seem pretty daft to you.'

'No dafter than if the most beautiful film star in the world wanted to marry me. But about as daft.'

His grin disappeared.

'I know!' he said, throwing up his arms in disgust and sending his jacket flying.

He swore, picked it up, and put it on.

'But I've got no choice. I have to know where I stand, otherwise it's no go.'

'What's no go?' I said.

'I'll tell you later. But anyhow, it's straight. Let's walk for a bit.'

We turned into the rue d'Alésia, and as soon as we got going he began to speak in such a rapid whisper I could scarcely catch what he said.

'First we need to know where we stand with each other,' he began. 'That explains all the jiggery-pokery. It wasn't just for the fun of it. You proved you trusted me when you came and met me on my terms. I think I can let you in on the job, but I'm a perfectionist. And I've got scruples. I want everything to be straight down the line between us. There's a lot at stake and without your help it'll slip through my fingers. But I want *you* to be able to trust *me*, too. I know you, Burma—'

'Saubert,' I corrected.

'Yes.'

He bit his lip and cast an anxious look round. But the street ran straight and empty in both directions, the lamps among the overhanging plane trees casting leafy shadows on the pavement, alternating with patches of bluish gloom. A traffic light at an intersection changed from red to green and back again despite the lack of traffic.

'Yes . . . Saubert,' Ferrand repeated. 'That's safer for the moment.'

'Respectable, too,' I said, smiling. 'It's the name of my income tax inspector.'

'I know you're straight,' he went on. 'And scrupulous. Like me. I know if I don't hide anything from you, you won't try to play any tricks on me.'

He stood very still for a second.

'I'm going to expose myself completely.'

'Not here!' I cried. 'Supposing somebody came along! What would they think?'

My joke left him cold as ice. He was well equipped for the hot weather.

'No. Not here,' he said. 'We'll go to my place. I want you to know everything about me.'

'Is this all part of the scenario?'

'Yes.'

'How many parts are there?'

'At least four.'

He started counting up on his fingers.

'First the accidental meeting in the bar. Then I meet you again in the street, waiting to tap me for some more money. Then I take you to my place, and give you a pair of shoes that are too small for me.'

He somehow managed to drop his voice even lower.

'Then if they see us together there's no harm done. You're just a down-and-out I can't get rid of.'

'They?' I said. 'Who's they?'

'People.'

He moved on again through the alternate light and shadow, by walls still warm from the sun.

'People you don't trust?'

He hesitated.

'People I don't want getting mixed up in the job.'

I made a fist, then straightened up one finger after another as if I was playing *mora*, the Italian thieves' game.

'One, two, three,' I said. 'Where's the fourth part?'

'Later,' he said.

I shrugged.

'Think yourself lucky you've come across someone as good-natured as I am. Anyone else would have sent you packing long ago.'

'But I didn't go to anyone else,' he said gravely. 'I need someone out of the ordinary, someone tough. And you're the one.'

I bowed.

'I'm flattered. But which of us is the crazier? Me for doing what you say like an idiot, or you for making everything so complicated? There was a perfectly safe and simple way of letting me know about this mysterious business. You could have come and exposed yourself completely, as you put it, in my office.'

'Not likely! I've told you – I wanted to know if I could trust you, and give you proof that *you* could trust *me*. There's more than a week's pocket money at stake here, mate.'

'How much?'

'A few hundred thousand.'

I started. He couldn't be talking about blackmailing Gaudebert. He'd never get that much out of him.

'You're joking!' I said.

'Word of honour.'

'And you say there's nothing crooked about it!'

'It couldn't be straighter.'

I sighed.

'Was it the nick or the loony bin you just got let out of?'

'The nick,' he said, then laughed. 'May be it'll come to the other place some day.'

'Sooner than you think if you keep on like this. Come on, let's go to your place then. A few hundred thousand is worth a little stroll. Is it far?'

'Rue Blottière.'

He clenched his fists and spat.

'A filthy hovel in the filthiest house in a filthy street,' he growled. 'But the bedbugs are clean. As shiny as ladybirds.'

I just hoped they were a bit smaller.

The last time I'd heard about the rue Blottière was in 1938. Three pieces of meat unfit for human consumption were found there and subsequently identified as the trunk, right arm and left thigh of an old lady who had completely lost her head. At the time it was an ideal setting for the fine art of human butchery. Things have improved since then – at least as regards town planning – though there are still some picturesque relics. The building Ferrand rented a room in, for example. It really was the sordid hole he'd described.

The two cramped floors seemed plunged in sleep or sinister suspense. The rotting façade overlooked an abandoned building site; the back faced on to a goods line. Among the many laws it defied was the law of gravity: despite many wooden props, it looked as if the first strong gust of wind would bring it down. Between the buttresses and the wall they propped up grew dusty thickets of reeking vegetation, typical of all the waste lands on the outskirts of the city. Keeping a bleary watch over the door stood an ancient street-lamp, still lit by gas. There aren't many of them left, and when you do see one you're always surprised not to see a body swinging from it. A revolting smell of decay, intensified by the heat, came wafting out of the entrance as we went in.

Strange as it may seem, this cockroach trap did have electricity. There's no stopping progress. My companion flicked on a time-switch hidden away somewhere, and an anaemic glow appeared over the stairs. Just enough to let you find the first step without putting your foot on the banana skin that lay there.

'You can come up,' said Ferrand in a noticeably louder voice. 'I'll give you the shoes and then you can make yourself scarce. We may have been POWs together, but still . . .'

I didn't answer. He was the star of the show, not me, and although I'd auditioned in the café I hadn't yet seen the rest of the script.

The rickety handrail was so filthy it was sticky to the touch, and the stairs were more like shelves, each exhibiting its rubbish: chewed fag-ends, burnt-out matches, old scraps of cotton wool, crumpled cigarette packets. The dung-coloured walls of this charming residence were decorated with obscene graffiti. Only over-the-hill crooks like Ferrand, or immigrants, or overweight tarts, would live in a dump like this. Though it was hard to believe any woman, however down on her luck, would put up with it. I understood why my friend with the tattoo was prepared to do anything to change his life style.

I was mistaken about the overweight part. I do make mistakes sometimes. We bumped into a redhead on the first-floor landing. The second redhead in the space of a few hours. Maybe it was written in my stars.

She was coming out of a dark bedroom with an empty wine bottle in her hand, as if on her way to replace it with a full one. A burnt-out cigarette dangled from her lips, and she wasn't too steady on her feet. When she saw us she flattened herself against the wall.

I wouldn't have given her much more than thirty. She had very pretty copper-coloured hair. It was in good condition, though in urgent need of a comb, and her last visit to the hairdresser couldn't have been that long ago. A rebellious lock hid one eye, but the rest cascaded over her shoulders. The eye I could see was that of a drunk or a drug addict. She was of medium height with a slender, sensuous nose and well-defined, generous lips. It must have been a very pleasant face when the signs of drunkenness wore off, but those looks wouldn't last long on a diet of cheap wine.

She was wearing worn old slippers and a dirty red dressing-gown, carelessly tied with a cord that didn't match. The tip of a firm, rounded breast peeped archly through the gap. Not at all the half-filled tobacco-pouch I'd have expected to find here.

I was suddenly overcome by a sense of unreality. Something didn't fit. I couldn't say what. Maybe just the slightest trace of a previous elegance; no more than a hint. I had a strange impression, as in a dream, that I was in the presence of a ghost. A ghost that had got itself into the wrong castle. And there was something else. My thoughts were irresistibly drawn to the other redhead, the girl in the rue du Douanier, the wife or its equivalent of M. Gaudebert. I shook my head. Something was amiss.

The redhead hiccuped something indistinguishable and tried to straighten her clothes. She did it so clumsily that her belt came undone and dropped to the floor at her feet. Her dressing-gown fell open, revealing that all she had on below the waist was a pair of stockings. Quite understandable in this weather. The stockings were full of ladders. She spat out a very graphic oath – so much for the trace of elegance – and nearly fell flat as she picked up the cord. Then she adjusted her dress as best she could, turned her back on us and went back into her room, slamming the door so violently she nearly brought the house down. There was a crash of broken glass. The bottle must have slipped out of her hand.

# 4 The rat of Montsouris

Ferrand lived on the same floor as the girl. I followed him into his room and he turned on the light. The bulb hanging from the ceiling cast as pale a light over the miserable scene as the first one had on the stairs. Ideal for the bedbugs' weak eyes.

'Who was she?' I asked.

Ferrand silently locked the door, then drew a moth-eaten old curtain over it.

'I don't know,' he said.

'Strange,' I said. 'She's grubby, badly dressed – as far as one could see! – and sozzled. And yet she doesn't seem to fit in here.'

'So,' he growled, gesturing at the room. 'And what about me? Do I fit in?'

I didn't answer.

I'd seen lavatories bigger than this place. A wash-stand, an iron bed and a rickety chair with a broken seat took up all the space. Someone with agoraphobia would have liked it.

Ferrand closed the window overlooking the railway line, shutting out the rattle of a goods train and shutting in a moth which at once began to flutter round the ailing light.

'But things are going to change,' he said.

He stood squarely in front of me.

'I've stumbled on something.'

I smiled.

'A lucky charm?'

'I said a few hundred thousand, remember?'

'I'm always hearing such things,' I said. 'And you're so long spitting it out—'

'All in good time,' he said. 'Have a seat.'

He set an example by flopping down on the bed.

I pulled the chair towards me and sat on it gingerly. It was more solid than I thought.

'Well?' I said.

The room was so cramped our faces were almost touching. We inhaled one another's breath.

'Ever heard of the Rats of Montsouris?' he said.

'Yes,' I said. 'My friend Marc Covet, a reporter on the *Crépuscule*, coined the name in one of his articles. They're thieves who operate mostly in this district, aren't they? The avenue du Parc-Montsouris, the rue de la Tombe-Issoire, and so on. What about them?'

He thumbed his hollow chest.

'I'm one of them,' he said.

'Really?' I said. 'And what are you telling me for?'

'So that you'll trust me.'

'I see. What do you want to do, turn them all in?'

He brandished a bony fist an inch from my nose.

'What do you take me for? That's not my style, you should know that. Not that I have much time for them – far from it . . . But I wouldn't grass on anyone.'

He took off his jacket and put it down beside him on the bed, then plucked a dingy handkerchief from his pocket, mopped his brow, and started wringing his hands again. He was getting more and more nervous. To tell the truth I was mopping my own brow: it was stifling in this rabbit hutch.

'To think I've fallen so low,' he said bitterly. 'A fifth-rate burglar. And I used to be such a flashy dresser, remember? Always loaded, too, thanks to my two birds. And now look at me.'

There must have been some space left on the floor because he spat into it.

'Listen, mate,' he went on. 'I did five years at Fresnes. Haven't been out long. And only to find I'd got it all wrong and the two dames had slung their hook. After that . . . You've heard from your reporter friends about loyalty among friends in the underworld, haven't you?'

I smiled.

He gave me a hangdog look.

'You catch on fast,' he said. 'Yes, it's a load of old rubbish.'

He leaned back and stared at the ceiling as if calling it to bear witness to man's inhumanity to man. The moth was still flapping round the light. Twice it cast a shadow across Ferrand's upturned face.

'A load of old rubbish,' he repeated. 'They all dropped me like a hot potato. Things were so bad I thought myself lucky when I came across someone else in the same fix. If it hadn't been for him I'd have had to get some lousy job.'

'What was his racket?'

'He was one of the Rats, as your reporter calls them.'

'So since then you've been breaking and entering?'

'Yes.'

'That can't bring in much.'

'Hell, no.'

'Are there many of you in this gang?'

He waved his hand again.

'This business is nothing to do with them.'

'Well, what is it to do with, for God's sake? If I have to ask you one more time I'll get lockjaw!'

He leaned forward.

'It's no ordinary job, let me tell you. And I don't want the Rats of Montsouris mixed up in it. First because they're dim, and second because I don't need them. But *you*—'

'What about me?'

He smiled.

'You're just the man for the job.'

'I'm sure I am,' I laughed. 'I can KO any mystery. And there's certainly plenty of mystery.'

'So it's no ordinary business,' he said again. 'Right. Now you know everything.'

'What!'

'I mean you know all about *me*,' he said. 'Look, mate, I'm an ex-con. You know what I'm up to. You know where I live. If you want to, you can put the cops on to me. I wanted to show you I trusted you and I thought this was the best way to do it. I'll tell you the rest another time. But not here. Don't look at me like that – I have my reasons. I'll phone you. Tomorrow at the latest.'

'To fix another meeting?'

'Well . . .'

'I'm not sure I'd come, another time.'

'I'll come to your place then.'

'You could have saved us both a lot of energy by doing that in the first place.'

'I wanted there to be a basis of mutual confidence,' he said, as if we were a couple of politicians.

'I'm not sure you succeeded.'

He shrugged.

'Too bad. But there's nothing crooked about it. You don't know what we'll be missing if you won't go along.'

'Oh yes I do,' I said. 'A few hundred thousand.'

'Yes.'

'Right,' I said. 'Brevity is the soul of wit, and this joke's gone on long enough to make a train for the queen of England.'

I stood up. Should I say anything about his attempt to blackmail Gaudebert? That certainly wasn't what had made him get me here. He must be so desperate he'd got several schemes going at once. If he found out I knew about this other one it wouldn't loosen his tongue. Just the opposite. Better to wait.

'Right,' I said. 'I'm off.'

He bent down and pulled a battered cardboard box from under the bed.

'Here are the shoes,' he said.

'Oh, yes,' I laughed. 'The alibi. Well, don't blame me if you find you still want them.'

I put the box under my arm.

'See you,' I said.

'See you,' he replied.

It didn't take him long to show me out. He pressed the time-switch of the light on the landing, we shook hands, and I left.

I didn't meet anyone on the way down. The whole house seemed ominously quiet.

It was just the same outside. The moon had risen, bathing everything in a sallow light that made it look even more baleful.

I crossed the road and waited in the shadows, gazing at the decrepit façade that sheltered a desirable female drunk and a somewhat less desirable ex-con. There was no sense in standing and staring like this. I wouldn't learn anything. It was just a reflex.

When the light in the stairway went off I set off for surroundings more attractive. My bathroom, for instance.

A bit further on I opened the box. I didn't expect to find shoes in it – been letting my imagination run away with me. They were still in reasonable condition, but I had no use for them. I was just about to chuck them over a fence when I saw two feet sticking out on to the pavement.

I went closer.

No, it wasn't a dead body. Just a live tramp, but dead drunk. One wine bottle had rolled into the gutter, and he was clutching a second one to his bosom. His shirt was open, his trousers immodestly undone and his feet exposed to the four winds. He'd rolled up his jacket and a raincoat of sorts into a pillow, but his head lay on the ground beside it in brutish sleep. Ferrand's shoes would be luxuries to him, so I grinned and put them down beside him, then went off feeling quite pleased with myself.

I'd been careful not to use up what little air there was by smoking in Ferrand's room, so now I lit my pipe.

Then, slowly, without quite knowing why, I retraced my steps. Was it because of the redhead or because of the man with the tattoo? I think, on the whole, it was because of the redhead.

I wasn't far from the house when a piercing cry shattered the silence.

# 5 Red for danger

A train on the nearby railway line threw up dense clouds of white steam, throwing a momentary veil across the moon. Then, with a metallic screech, it faded into the distance. No other sound. No other cry. No shutter thrown open, not a single curious face peering out from a window.

Unless I was mistaken the sound had come from Ferrand's building. I stuffed my pipe in my pocket and sprinted through the dank hall and up the stairs two at a time, not bothering to look for the light switch. But I didn't get far. Someone was standing motionless and silent in the darkness, and I ran straight into them.

I tried instinctively to grab hold of whoever it was, but got a kick in the belly which though it couldn't have been aimed was enough to make me lose my balance and fall down backwards to the bottom of the stairs. I tried to fall like a cat so as not to hit my head on the concrete floor. But I'm not a cat.

Someone jumped over me with what sounded like a rustle of wings. I was too shaken to do anything about it. When I came to, after a few seconds, I got to my feet and swore. My hand was still cool from contact with a firm round breast that still didn't go with this house.

I struck a match.

The bosom in question and all that went with it had

gone. I was alone, terribly alone, with my head spinning and the stairway strewn with garbage. An old slipper had now joined the collection, amid the obscene graffiti and the dense, oppressive silence.

What a place to live. Every man for himself and the devil take the hindmost. Ears wide open. Mouths and doors tight shut.

I felt my way silently upstairs, stopped outside Ferrand's door and listened. Silence. Plus heat and stench. I gave the door a push and it creaked open. I groped for the light-switch and flicked it on. The moth started to bump madly round the pale bulb again.

It seemed to have got bigger. Its huge, fantastic shadow flicked back and forth across the gaunt face of the Rat of Montsouris. It made him look as if he was still alive.

'*I've stumbled on something.*'

'*A lucky charm?*'

He was resting more or less in peace on the floor. On his back, with his feet by the head and his head by the foot of the bed. If the razor had slashed a fraction deeper the head might have been yards away. It was only just attached to the body. The work of an expert; it made me think of the colonies.

Blood everywhere. Its sickly, cloying smell was almost overpowering by now. A sizzling noise: the moth had flown too close to the light bulb. It fell right into the wound in Ferrand's throat, and fluttered there for a few seconds like a vampire quenching its thirst. Then it too died.

I suddenly realized I might soon make a third. I reached for my shooter, and swore under my breath. I hadn't brought it with me. The darkness out on the landing seemed to press in on me. I turned to look. No sign of anyone. I quietly closed the door and stood staring down at Ferrand – I still don't know why. Perhaps to give myself time to recover. There was nothing much to be done for him except recite the prayers for the dead, and I don't know them. It would be difficult to search him because of all the gore. His shirt and trousers looked saturated. Then I realized it would be useless anyway. His trouser pockets were turned inside out: they'd been searched already. I looked for the jacket he'd laid on the bed. It had disappeared. The best thing I could do was follow its example before something nasty happened.

I took out my handkerchief and wiped the back of the chair and the light-switch, then turned off the light and beat a hasty retreat. I reached the street without mishap. Nobody followed me. Nobody tried anything. It wasn't really such a dangerous place after all.

I got to the avenue du Maine without a hitch, via the passage Bournisien and the rue Vercingétorix. There were still two or three bars open in the rue de la Gaîté, where I'd parked my car earlier in the evening. But I walked past them, climbed into the car, and set off for home sweet home.

When I first noticed the smell of blood, driving along, I thought it was my imagination. But as soon as I got into my bedroom I saw my jacket was spattered with it. And it was still wet. That made me think. The stains couldn't have got there while I was in Ferrand's room: I'd stayed at a respectful distance from the body for that very reason.

Perhaps it wasn't some immigrant who'd arranged that tableau.

I could only have picked up the stains when I brushed against the redhead during our second meeting on the stairs. And if she'd had blood on her dressing-gown . . .

I had a cold drink to freshen myself up, took a sleeping pill to calm myself down, then went to bed. Starkers. Like the redhead. Then I swore. I'd just had an idea. But it was a bit too late. *L'esprit d'escalier*, you might say.

# 6 Some conversations

I woke up a few hours later, saying to myself:

'When it came to the crunch the 'tec lacked punch!'

You get your best ideas in the morning, as Rimbaud used to say. But this one was almost over. It was nearly eleven, and today was going to be as hot as yesterday. I got up and tried to fight off the effects of the sleeping pill. I cleaned up the stained jacket as best I could, and hid it. Then I washed and dressed, slipped my shooter into my pocket – you wouldn't find me anywhere without it from now on – and set off for the Fiat Lux Detective Agency.

'There you are at last!' exclaimed *la belle Hélène* as I came in. She was as beautiful as ever. 'I was going to give you five more minutes before I called you.'

I aimed my hat at its peg, and missed.

'Is that so?' I said. 'What should the first thing be that you say to your boss?'

'Morning, boss,' she said.

'Morning, sweetie. Why were you going to call me? Has an anxious client turned up?'

'I was wondering what had happened to you.'

I sat down.

'Were you worried?' I asked.

'Just wondering,' she said, running her fingers carelessly – oh, so carelessly – through her wild chestnut hair.

'I went to bed late,' I said. 'And I've just got up. I only finished shaving ten minutes ago.'

'I didn't ask for details.'

I stroked my cheek.

'I'm giving them to you anyway,' I said. 'Ten minutes, that's all.'

'So what?' she said.

I shrugged.

'No one would think I'd taught you deductive reasoning. Never mind. I don't care for that lipstick of yours. It comes off.'

I winced. A pain in my back reminded me I'd been practising my gliding. I stood up and rubbed my ribs.

'What's the matter?' said Hélène. 'Rheumatism? Only to be expected at your time of life.'

'I've been taking violent exercise with a redhead,' I said.

'A redhead? Not the—'

'No. Another one.'

"How many do you need?' she asked. 'That's another thing you should be careful of at your age. You really oughtn't to be let out on your own. You were supposed to be meeting an ex-fellow-prisoner and part-time blackmailer called Ferrand.'

Swearing is excellent therapy. The pain had gone. I sat down again.

'There was a redhead as well,' I said.

She gave me a mischievous glance.

'Does her lipstick come off too?'

'Many a true word, Hélène, my love,' I said, seriously now. 'She left red marks in a big way. And now, as you decline to kiss me and it would be silly to bear a grudge about it, let's get down to business.'

I waited a moment.

'Ferrand's dead,' I said. 'Enough blood for half the slaughterhouses in Paris.'

'My God!' she gasped.

Then she tossed her head prettily.

'Just as I was saying,' she sighed. 'You shouldn't be let out on your own. You'll never change. How did it happen?'

'Not quite the same way as usual. Normally when I arrange to meet someone who's going to die, he's dead when I turn up. Ferrand was killed after I met him.'

'And I suppose you know who did it?'

'You say it as though you had some idea.'

'Well . . .'

'Gaudebert, eh?' I said. 'Of course. Ferrand's blackmailing him, so he hires me to give Ferrand a fright. But then he decides that the best way to dispose of him is to bump him off. And as he hasn't lopped a head off for a long time he gets hold of a razor and does the job himself.'

'Don't make fun of me,' she said sulkily.

'Why not?' I said. 'It's good for the nerves. Listen, Hélène. Old Ferrand had a quite legitimate desire to improve his lot. But he lived dangerously. He had several fiddles going at once, and one of them misfired. Maybe he was killed by one of the other Rats of Montsouris, maybe by the drunken redhead, or maybe by someone else. Maybe it was to do with the business he wanted to involve me in; maybe it wasn't. And now that I've run out of maybes, I'll tell you exactly what happened last night.'

'Well,' she said when I'd finished. 'You haven't got much to go by. Only Ferrand's claim that his plan was worth several hundred thousand francs and it wasn't crooked.'

'Yes. And if I go on being as stupid as I was last night I'm not likely to find out any more. That kick I got on the stairs must have scrambled my neurons.'

I thumped on the table.

'Now, now,' said Hélène soothingly. 'Don't get worked up. You mean because you ran off when you saw Ferrand had been killed, instead of searching the building? What good would that have done? Playing the hero's all very well, but—'

'I'm not talking about playing the hero,' I said. 'I know when and when not to do that. I'd no idea what I'd got myself involved in and I didn't have a gun, so I thought I'd better not go any further without giving things a bit of thought. But there was a way I could've found out more without too much risk – even if it was the lady who took the razor to Ferrand.'

'Lady?' Hélène said.

'The red chick,' I said. 'Red hair, and blood on her clothes. Any fool would have thought of it. But of course I'm not just any fool.'

'What *ought* you to have thought of then?' she said.

'She was starkers under her dressing-gown,' I said. 'And she lost a shoe when she landed that kick. She couldn't get far like that. I ought to have got my car and gone after her. I'd have winkled her out somehow.'

'Well, don't shed too many tears,' said Hélène. 'You're right about that fall – it did scramble your brains. If she ran away with nothing on but a dressing gown she must have had somewhere to hide. One of the nearby houses, no doubt. You could have scoured the neighbourhood till you were blue in the face, you wouldn't have found her.'

I shook my head.

'No, that can't be right,' I said. 'I still think she didn't belong in that dump and isn't from that part of town.'

'Supposing—' Hélène said, then stopped herself.

'Yes?'

'Supposing she'd been kidnapped? Supposing she was being kept there against her will?'

My back gave another twinge. I began to rub it again.

'She seemed pretty free,' I said.

'Particularly with her legs,' said my secretary with a sly smile. 'Anyhow, if she went walking around Plaisance in that state . . . Rather a pretty name, Plaisance, don't you think?'

'I'll ask Ferrand when I see him,' I said. 'He's sure to have an opinion.'

'Anyhow if she went walking around Plaisance in the altogether, she was probably picked up by the police. I'm going down to get the first edition of the evening papers. Maybe they'll mention it. *"Mystery girl wanders through torrid night naked but for bloodstained dressing-gown."* That's the kind of headline reporters can't resist if they've got something to put underneath.'

'Underneath?' I said. 'There were some delightful items underneath.'

Hélène blushed and rustled off, leaving me alone with the scent of her perfume, the smell of my pipe, a pain in the back and a puzzled mind.

She was soon back with *France-Soir, Paris-Presse* and the *Crépuscule*. But there was no mention in any of them of *'Mystery girl wanders through torrid night, etc.'* Nor of *'Unknown man found with throat slashed in 14th arrondissement,'* which you'd have thought would be equally appealing.

'H'm' I said. 'Rather strange, don't you think?'

'What do you mean? I must have been right. Someone gave the woman shelter nearby. As for the body, they're often not found for some time.'

'Perhaps you're right,' I said.

I picked up the phone, called the *Crépuscule*, and finally got through to Marc Covet.

After the usual courtesies I asked:

'Nothing for the morning edition, is there, about a young woman on the loose in Paris in her birthday suit?'

'Birthday suit, eh?' he said, no doubt with a leer. 'Is she the one that got away?'

'Almost,' I said.

'Not a blonde arsonist, by any chance?'

'Pretty hot.'

'But is she a blonde?' he insisted.

'No, a redhead. Have you got anything?'

'No,' he said.'And they'd have caught something as sensational as that, especially at this time of the year. Is this the start of something?'

'Could be,' I said.

'Any crumbs for me?'

'The usual,' I said. 'If you can make yourself useful.'

'I'll do my best – keep my eye on what's coming up. When and where did it happen?'

'Last night in the Plaisance area,' I said.

'Plaisance, eh? News from round there usually comes in fast. She hadn't come out of that house, had she?'

So they'd found Ferrand's body, I thought. And Marc had connected it with the girl straight off. Quick on the uptake, young Marc.

'What house?' I asked as casually as possible.

'Of course there's no reason why you should have heard about it,' he said. 'Some house caught fire around there. And when there's a woman wandering the streets naked and a house in flames nearby, you're bound to assume the former left the latter in a hurry.' He laughed. 'Especially when she's a fiery redhead!'

'Stop playing the fool,' I said. 'My fiery redhead didn't come out of any burning building. But I've got an idea. Maybe she was picked up by the cops and they haven't told the press because she belongs to an influential family.'

'Influential family?' exclaimed Marc. 'In Plaisance?'

'She may be from a posher part of town.'

'This is getting interesting,' he said.

'Anyway,' I said. 'It should have come in on the ticker at Police Headquarters. Could you check it with the bloke in charge?'

'As it happens, he's in the next-door office,' said Marc. 'Hang on.'

I waited a good minute with the phone to my ear and my mind churning. Then he was back.

'Damn all,' he said.

'Never mind,' I said. 'Thanks all the same. What's all this about a house burning down?'

'Some dump caught fire early this morning. Not surprising. One cigarette end in this heat and the die is cast.'

'You do have a way with words,' I said.

'I'm quoting from a colleague. But the purple prose won't get past the sub. The whole thing only rates a couple of lines. Who gives a curse what happens in the rue Blottière?'

I started.

'Quite,' I said. 'Still, it's not every day you can have a charity ball to spread yourselves on, is it?'

'More's the pity!' he said, and hung up.

'I'm going back to prowl around a bit,' I said after bringing Hélène up to date. 'Why don't you come along? We can stop somewhere round there for lunch.'

# 7 Flight of the rats

I drew up under the railway bridge which marks the boundary between the 13th and 14th arrondissements, and after which the rue de Gergovie becomes the rue de la Procession. I think it's called the Pont de la Procession, but I couldn't swear to it. I got out and tinkered with the engine a bit. With the aid of an old phone directory I'd discovered there was a small garage in the rue Blottière, so a break-down would give me a good excuse for being in the area, should I need one. When I'd finished scene-setting I left Hélène to look after the car and went the rest of the way on foot.

Life's full of surprises. Creaking doors hang the longest. There *had* been a fire in the rue Blottière, but not where I'd thought. The house where Ferrand met his end was still there as large as life, looking no less run down in the daytime than it had at night. As a matter of fact, the sunshine made the whole ramshackle affair, with its crumbling walls and clumsy buttresses, look even more decrepit.

I went into the garage and explained my situation to a man in greasy blue overalls. I pretended to be a weekend driver, so he piled on the possible costs and summoned a lad in a baseball cap. Between them they got the break-down truck out of its shed and we all set off. When we reached the car they didn't even bother to see what the trouble was – just hitched it up to the truck without a word and back we all went to the garage. There they treated themselves to a glass of wine before getting down to work. They'd have asked Hélène to join them, given half a chance.

'Will it take long?' I asked.

The man in blue overalls scratched the back of his neck. 'You can never tell,' he said.

'Right,' I said. 'We'll go for a stroll while we're waiting.'

'Not much to see round here,' he said.

'Unless they've let Julot out of the cells,' laughed the lad with the baseball hat. 'But he's not a pretty sight for a lady.'

'Who's Julot?' I asked.

'The local drunk. When he's plastered, instead of going home he sleeps on the pavement in his clothes. Or rather, out of them. The cops carted him off this morning for indecent exposure. No trousers. He says someone nicked them and his old raincoat while he was asleep. That's why I said he's not a suitable sight for a lady.'

He leered towards the doorway as he said this, and I turned too, and started to laugh. Hélène was standing at the entrance to the garage, with the sun shining through her dress and showing any man worth the name what excellent legs she was endowed with.

I leant towards the baseball cap.

'Nice chassis, eh, son?'

'First rate,' he agreed. 'Some people have all the luck.'

Then he started to blush like a girl. He didn't have the legs though.

'Careful,' I said. 'Your cheeks will catch light. Talking of which, it seems there's been a fire in this street?'

'Yes. Over there,' said the other man, pointing vaguely.

'Serious?' I said.

'Quite. No one hurt, though,' said the boy in the cap.

His eyes wandered in search of Hélène again, but she'd caught on and moved out of sight.

The youth sighed.

'They're all the same,' I consoled him. 'Selfish to the marrow.'

'One nest of bedbugs the less,' said the man in the overalls. I wasn't quite sure what he meant, so I was relieved when he added: 'There are a few more houses round here that could do with a good fire to clean them out.'

'Yes,' I said. 'That dump I noticed on the way here, for example. But I don't live round here myself, so I wouldn't want to criticize—'

'Don't worry – I only work here,' said the man in overalls. 'Which house do you mean?'

'The one with the wooden props just about holding it up. With an old gas-lamp over the door.'

'I know the one,' he said. 'They've been talking about demolishing it for years. But they'll wait for it to fall down by itself.'

'Does anyone live there?' I said.

'Apparently it's quite comfortable inside,' he answered. 'It's the outside that's the problem. And it's the outside that counts, isn't it? I haven't actually been in to see, of course.'

'See what?' I said.

'Whether you could really live there. There's some Arab in there, and one or two other fellows who aren't supposed to be too friendly. And a bird, too. They must share her between them. Anyhow, they're not very sociable. So it's better for other people not to be too curious, don't you think?'

This might have been a warning. I changed the subject.

'Right,' I said. 'We'll go for a walk while you repair the car.'

'Enjoy yourselves,' he said.

I joined Hélène and we made our way, not too obviously, towards the house where the crime had taken place.

'This is nudists' corner,' I said as we approached. 'The redhead didn't hide nearby. She went back home, some distance away, decently if not very elegantly dressed, having pinched the trousers and raincoat off a drunk of my acquaintance. And I'd just left a pair of shoes beside him. They must have come in useful too.'

'What about the dressing-gown?' said Hélène.

'She can't have left it behind in exchange. It would have been noticed, with all that blood on it, and those two at the garage would have heard about it. She must have got rid of it on the way home, down a drain or on a patch of waste land.'

There were wild yells and the sound of galloping feet behind us, and four kids playing cowboys and Indians shoved past us and disappeared through an opening in a fence a few yards further on. They soon set up a terrific din, drumming on old pots and pans.

'There it is,' I said, pointing to the house.

'It certainly is in a state.'

'But still standing. Less dramatic, perhaps, than smoking ruins, but more useful if we ever want any fingerprints.'

'And you're sure there are people actually living there?' she said with a grimace.

'The man at the garage confirmed my own theory,' I said. 'People who keep themselves to themselves – and one of them's an Arab. That probably means there's a razor not far away. And there's a bird they take turns with.'

Hélène blushed.

'It looks completely deserted now, anyhow,' she said.

'I shouldn't count on it. That's how it looked before. Do you feel brave enough to come with me?'

'You're not going to—'

'Yes, I am. There's nothing to be afraid of. It's broad daylight and they probably did all they had to last night.

Come on. We're a young married couple looking for a love nest, and with the housing shortage what it is . . .'

The hall reeked with its now familiar essence of zoo. There was a dim light on the stairs thanks to a narrow slit of a window, its dusty panes miraculously still intact, which I hadn't noticed on my first visit. There seemed to be even more rubbish than before. As well as crumpled bits of paper and cigarette ends there were now pieces of straw, and it looked as if the dust from a sack of coal had been scattered on some of the treads.

'Concierge!' I called, just for form's sake. I knew perfectly well there wasn't a concierge, but a shout might bring someone else out.

But no one answered.

'Let's go up,' I said.

I went up to the first floor, Hélène behind me. If there was anyone there they were keeping very quiet about it. Silence was the speciality of the house. Muffled sounds drifted in from outside: children larking about on the waste lot, men working on the railway line.

For the sake of appearances I knocked on the other doors on the first-floor landing. No result. Hélène's expression clearly said:

'Empty, just as I thought.'

It certainly looked like it. I went over to Ferrand's door and turned the tarnished brass handle. The door swung open.

The bedside table and the chair were piled up in one corner. The iron bedstead was up-ended against the wall. But there was no corpse lying on the floor. It had vanished, taking with it all dust, all litter, and all trace of blood.

'It's been cleaned up,' said Hélène.

'Thoroughly. The only place there could be any clues is between the floor-boards. If clues are needed it'll be a job for the lab.'

'Are you going to tell Commissaire Faroux?' she asked.

'Not till I think it's necessary,' I said. 'Anyhow, there's no point in hanging around. Ferrand didn't write the name of his murderer or murderess on the wall, or leave the address of his next of kin. Let's try next door. No point in having scruples now.'

We went into all the rooms on that floor. The one the redhead had burst out of with a wine bottle was the first of a three-room flat. One room looked out on the street, and two on the railway line and several piles of coal. The architect who designed the house had obviously studied with Doctor Caligari. A more cock-eyed layout could hardly be imagined. Le Corbusier would have swallowed his plumbline at the sight of it. Some rickety bits of furniture played hide and seek in the corners, and empty bottles stood about like skittles. I opened some drawers. As noisy as politicians' speeches, and as empty.

I leaned out of the window overlooking the railway line. Below, what had once been a few square yards of garden running down to the embankment was now overrun with the sinister weeds already mentioned. But no one was there to throw a piece of information, or even a stone, my way. There wasn't even a corpse.

I joined Hélène in the next room.

'Well, I must say!' I laughed.

She started. Her cheeks were so flushed you could have fried an egg on them. She'd been contemplating the head of a bed which looked about as comfortable as Ferrand's, but which was ornamented with a collection of the sort of pictures strictly forbidden – heaven knows why – to good little girls. They represented a highly stimulating range of bosoms and buttocks. Whoever slept there obviously cut out pin-ups from girlie magazines. But the prize exhibit wasn't a photo. It was an ink drawing by someone who'd used a real but peculiar artistic talent to produce what might at a pinch illustrate the menu for a wedding, but certainly not one for a first communion.

'Better and better,' I grinned, reaching over to unpin it.

'Leave it alone! Don't be so disgusting!' cried Hélène furiously, grabbing my arm.

But I already had my trophy.

'Don't you be so silly!' I replied. 'Let people practise their vices in peace. Look what your girlish modesty might have made us miss.'

A small oblong photo fluttered down on to the bed. It must have been stuck up behind one corner of the drawing and gradually slipped out of sight. I picked it up.

'More filth, I expect,' said Hélène.

'No, my love,' I said. 'This one's fully clothed. No less desirable, though. Especially as she seems to be sober.'

The photo had been taken by an expert with a very good camera. It showed a young woman with a pretty figure set off by an elegant dress. She had long shoulder-length hair, and was leaning gracefully against the parapet of a bridge over a single-line railway track. The sides of the cutting were planted with trees; the whole atmosphere seemed delightfully rural.

'The redhead herself,' I said, stowing both photo and drawing away in my pocket. 'The most careful crook always leaves something lying around. So now you see being broad-minded can have its advantages.'

Hélène shrugged and didn't answer. I gave her a friendly tap on the shoulder to tell her it was time to leave. I'd got more from the house than I'd dared hope for. We could do the same as the previous tenants: leave without a backward glance.

We went back to the garage and I went in alone. Hélène stayed outside, sulking.

'It's ready, monsieur,' said the mechanic in the blue overalls. 'Enjoy your walk?'

'Yes, thanks,' I said. 'Was there much wrong?'

'No. I suppose the lady was driving?'

'Yes,' I lied.

'That explains everything,' he said.

'How much do I owe you?'

He told me. The lad with the baseball cap came up looking for a tip. I gave him one, then showed him the photo.

'You've got an eye for the girls,' I said. 'Do you know this one, by any chance?'

'Pull the other one,' he said sadly. 'How would I know a girl like that?'

'I don't know. I found it lying on the pavement down the road. Thought it might be someone from round here.'

'Never set eyes on her.'

'What about the one with all the boy-friends in the house we were talking about this morning?'

'No!' he said. 'Not the same type at all.'

'Right,' I said. 'After all, it's no skin off my nose. I'll hang on to it. If no one has claimed it a year and a day from now, I'll stick it in my family album. She's obviously a country girl.'

'How do you make that out?'

'The setting,' I said.

He laughed.

'Are you from Paris?

'More or less.'

'Not from the 14th arrondissement, anyway! Do you know where that photograph was taken? On the bridge between the rue des Arbustes and the villa des Camélias, behind the Hôpital Broussais. I know that district like the back of my hand! I was born in the rue Didot and I live in the impasse Omnibus.'

'Oh! That's the old Outer Circle line, then?'

'That's right. Part of it still functions. You see goods

wagons go by sometimes late at night, transporting cars. From the factories at Javel to the Gare de Lyon, I think.'

You're always finding out something new about Paris. I lived for a number of years in the 14th arrondissement, first in the villa Duthy, in the same building as Jacques Prévert, then in the rue de Vanves, over the *Majestic-Brune*. Both places are close to the little street called the villa des Camélias, but I never even suspected its existence. Of course, it's not very easy to find.

I drove the Dugat out of the garage and picked up Hélène.

'So what have I got to do to stop you sulking?' I asked after a while.

'I'm not sulking,' she snapped.

'Sorry,' I said. 'My mistake. It must be my imagination. Well, you've seen what the girl looks like. We haven't wasted our time, have we? Let's go and give the area around that bridge the once-over. Perhaps the redhead's a Lady of the Camellias. Let's find out where she lives and how to approach her.'

I consulted a map of Paris.

'Good. This is my lucky day. The villa of the Camellias is within spitting distance of the rue des Mariniers, where Anatole Jakowski lives. You know, the chap Ralph Messac, the journalist, introduced me to a few months ago.'

'He's an art critic, isn't he?'

'Yes. He specializes in naïve painting. If the redhead lives thereabouts, Jakowski might be able to give us a lead on her. She's not the kind of girl to pass unnoticed.'

# 8 A lead on the redhead

I stopped the car at the end of the rue des Arbustes – almost next to the grey-painted gate that acts as a kind of stage door to the Hôpital Broussais, and just by the wall barring cars from the bridge that spans the old Outer Circle line and connects the rue des Arbustes with the villa des Camélias.

The man in the garage was right. The place was just as it appeared on the photograph: rural, picturesque and amazingly peaceful. You'd never have thought it was close to busy streets like the Boulevard Brune, the rue Didot and the rue de Vanves. There was a factory not far away, but you had to look hard to make out its long dark wall beyond the trees; the low hum of its machinery blended into the heaviness of the sultry afternoon. Only the birds were making a noise, but their twitter was restful and pleasant.

For about forty yards on either side of the foot-bridge the metal rails ran shining in the sun between steep banks covered with grass and trees. But at either end of this open stretch the line disappeared into a tunnel.

Here and there beside the track a broken vegetable crate or cardboard box lay abandoned to its fate. There was also a solitary shoe that had seen better days, and, caught on a mass of brambles, something resembling a pair of trousers. Some people in Paris have never heard of dustbins.

Faint pathways snaking among the trees showed that it was a favourite playground for children and trysting place for lovers.

Telling Hélène to wait by the car, I found a gap in the fence near the hospital gate, slipped through, and went down and across the track to the objects that had attracted my attention. I recognized the shoe at once. It was one of the pair Ferrand had given me. The trousers must have been the ones stolen from the sleeping wino. The raincoat couldn't be far away. But there was no point in looking for it. I knew all I needed to know.

I was about to cross the track again when Hélène shouted a warning.

I waved back reassuringly. I'd already felt the rail vibrate under my feet and seen the train. I stepped back, and a locomotive drawing a string of flat wagons laden with new car bodies wheezed past with a rush of hot air. The driver leaned out and shouted something at me, but it was lost in the clatter of the wheels, and the whole train was soon swallowed up in the tunnel.

I climbed back to Hélène.

'The redhead must live in the neighbourhood,' I said. 'She threw her disguise away in there. If it had been winter she'd have burned it, but boilers are out of action at this time of year. It'll be child's play to find out her address. We'll go and talk to Jakowski. If he doesn't know, we'll do the rounds of the shopkeepers and show them the photograph.'

After the foot-bridge the villa des Camélias ran along by the railway fence for a few yards. Then came a recess, with an old flight of five or six steps leading up to a mysterious door. After that the road turned and made straight for the passage Noirot. On every side there were small houses built in various styles, among them a couple of artists' studios. It was similar to the rue du Douanier over at Montsouris.

There were lots of flowers and creepers. Music could be heard playing quietly on a radio. From an empty flat somewhere came the strident sound of a telephone, and an irate watch-dog alternately tugged at his chain and snapped at flies.

We turned left into the passage Noirot, then right into the rue des Mariniers, where Anatole Jakowski lived. Through an open window full of lush potted plants came the business-like clicking of a typewriter. I rang the bell and the clicking stopped.

Jakowski opened the door.

'What a lucky coincidence!' he said, raising his velvet cap to Hélène, his little fair goatee all aquiver. 'Ralph Messac is here. Do come in. I was just putting the finishing touches to my book on Alphonse Allais.'

We followed him into his study. It was filled with naïve paintings, examples of *art nouveau*, and the other strange, more or less Surrealist, works that make up his large collection. The draught we made coming in set in motion one of Calder's earliest 'mobiles' where it stood between two tobacco jars in the form of human faces.

Ralph Messac leaned against the wall, a dignified and imposing figure with his beard and his exotic South American pipe. His hair was almost touching a statue of a Siren, once an object of admiration in the rue Mazarine in the house of the poet Robert Desnos.

'What's been going on in the 14th to bring you here?' he asked after we'd exchanged the usual greetings.

'Oh, you're pricking up your ears, are you?' laughed Jakowski. 'In that case I've got a good local example of black humour for you. A chap was just coming out of the Hôpital Broussais this morning – he'd been a patient there, but had been discharged cured – and he was run over by an ambulance. It was rushing back to the hospital with someone dying inside. So there were two corpses.'

He turned to Hélène.

'Our friend here keeps a record of all the incidents, from the sublime to the ridiculous, that take place in the 14th arrondissement.'

'An anthology of every day life, eh?' I laughed. 'Dogs getting run over, females fighting, houses being broken into, and so on. Talking of which, those burglaries around Montsouris must have given you something to get your teeth into.'

Messac carefully took his long pipe out of his mouth and blew a cloud of sweet-smelling smoke at two little men made of cork playing cards inside a bottle. As in honour bound, I took out my bull's head and got it going.

'I'm not interested in trivialities like that,' he said. 'Too ordinary. The episode Jakowski just told us about, yes. Or the amateur pot-holers who popped up right under the nose of a copper in the place Victor-Basch. They came bursting out of a manhole in the early hours of the morning, carrying their lamps and ropes and picks and other paraphernalia. The policeman couldn't believe his eyes. They'd deliberately got themselves locked into the catacombs so they'd have plenty of time to explore the underground passages that aren't open to the public!'

'Quite,' I said. 'But that's enough anecdotes. I know you two – once you get going we'll be here till midnight. Take a look at this!'

I took the photograph of the redhead out of my pocket and handed it to Jakowski.

'I've reason to believe she lives around here,' I said. 'Do you know her? It might not be obvious from this picture, but in the flesh she's very striking. Once seen never forgotten.'

'Of course I know her,' he said, tapping the photograph with his forefinger. '*Extremely* striking! If Mademoiselle weren't here' – he threw a sidelong glance at Hélène, who

was studying a cabinet full of turn-of-the-century curios –
'I'd go into detail, but in Poland . . .'

'Never mind Poland,' I said. 'Jarry said it doesn't exist.
Surely they teach you that at the College of Pataphysics?
What's more, the Poles are supposed to be permanently
sloshed, and you don't drink.'

'True enough.'

'You're a traitor, then. So forget Polish chivalry, and spit
it out!'

'All right,' he said. 'Her name's Marie—'

'Like the Blessed Virgin?'

'Goodness, no!'

'The Magdalen, then?'

'That's more like it. She's a nymphomaniac. Everyone
in the neighbourhood knows about her. She has these
attacks and runs wild. I believe they've tried psychiatric
treatment, but it didn't work.'

'She just jumps into bed with the first man she bumps
into, is that it?' I said.

'No. She only goes for low types. Once she chummed
up with a rag-and-bone man from the flea market. It took
her husband a week to track her down.'

'Oh, so she's married, is she?' I said.

'Yes. To a *very* respectable gent,' he said ironically.
'*Extremely* highly thought of. A painter. Grand Prix de
Rome and all that. Leading light of the *Salon*, semi-official
portraitist of public figures, recipient of government commissions.'

'Which only adds spice to the affair,' said Messac sarcasti-
cally.

'There was another scandal too, I remember,' Jakowski
went on. 'At a dance-hall in the rue de Pernety. It came
out because there was a police raid. But the husband smoothed it all over.'

'Does this husband happen to have a name?' I said.

'Auguste Courtenay.'

'And where do this modern couple live?' I asked.

'In the villa des Camélias.'

'What number?'

'I'm not sure. A Normandy-style house – grey stone, timbered, if you can see the wood for the ivy. A studio's been added, but it doesn't spoil the general appearance too much. And there's a garage built in the same style as the house.'

'Is there a big wrought-iron lamp by the front door?' I asked.

'Yes.'

'I noticed the place as we came past just now,' I said. 'It looked empty.'

'Well, I bumped into Courtenay yesterday,' said Jakowski. 'But come to think of it, our Marie might be up to her tricks again. I pass the house every day on my way to the market, and I nearly always see her at the window, usually half naked. But I haven't seen her for several days. Maybe she's gone off on one of her sprees. Or of course her husband might have murdered her. He'll do it one day. He's been threatening to for a long time.'

'Don't you think she might get in first?' I said.

'What do you mean?'

'*She* might kill *him*.'

'Don't worry,' he said. 'I saw him only yesterday, as I said. Alive and kicking.'

'Well, might she kill someone else, then?' I said. 'Look here, Jakowski, I'm going to speak frankly. I'm working for someone who's slept with her. A married man who temporarily lost his head, as they say. He doesn't know anything about her – name, address, age, nothing. But she left this photo at his house by accident. And he's got the wind up because according to him she's threatened to kill him. Is she the kind of woman to make such a threat? And to carry it out? Or is my client taking me for a ride?'

Jakowski shrugged.

'My dear fellow, I don't know. When you're dealing with someone who's mad you have to be ready for anything. And she drinks and takes drugs as well.'

'In other words,' I said, 'if you heard she'd killed someone you wouldn't be surprised?'

He thought for a moment. Then:

'No. I wouldn't be surprised,' he declared.

'Thank you,' I said. 'One other thing. You're an art critic. Have a look at this.'

I took back the photo of Marie Courtenay and held out the drawing I'd found with it.

'Aha!' said Ralph Messac quietly.

'Pretty, isn't it?' I said. 'What do you think, Jakowski?' He laughed.

'I'm chiefly interested in naïve artists, you know,' he said.

'This is hardly naïve, I agree,' I said. 'But would your friend Auguste Courtenay be likely to toss off stuff like this?'

'Anyone who's won the Prix de Rome, who exhibits regularly at the *Salon*, and who accepts commissions from the state is capable of anything,' he said. 'If only to restore his self-respect. But this drawing wasn't done by Courtenay.'

'Don't some artists manage to change their style to produce this kind of thing?'

'That's true. But something of their real technique always comes through. I don't think Courtenay did this. But of course I couldn't swear to it.'

'Right,' I said. 'Well, thank you.'

I got my drawing back with some difficulty, then asked:

'Is he well off – Courtenay?'

'Yes. No need to resort to this sort of thing to keep body and soul together, if that's what you mean.'

'No. I didn't mean that. I was just thinking that if he's rich the Romeos his wife digs up might try to blackmail him.'

Anatole Jakowski shook his head.

'They might try,' he said. 'But I doubt if he'd wear it. I once saw him beat up a young thug outside his house. You should've seen the trouncing he gave him. And I heard him say: "If you need a rest there's a hospital just down the road." The thug had probably been asking for a pay-off. You see, my dear Burma, his wife's behaviour can't harm his reputation any more. The damage is done. Mind you, he's an artist, and even the starchiest moralists allow artists and their nearest and dearest a certain amount of licence. They can get away with things a grocer, a general or a tax inspector couldn't. In other words, Courtenay isn't going to pay anyone to keep quiet about something that's general knowledge and can't do him any more harm.'

'Of course not,' I said. 'Thank you again. We'll leave you both to get on with Alphonse Allais.'

And we went through the ritual exchange of microbes again.

'Delighted to have made your acquaintance, M. Jakowski,' said Hélène in her prissiest voice as we all shook hands. 'I *have* enjoyed looking at your fascinating collection.'

Our host smiled modestly.

'That's nothing,' I said. 'Compared to what you'd have seen if he'd shown you his bust.'

'The most extraordinary thing you ever saw!' agreed Messac.

'If you want to see that,' said the writer-cum-art-critic, 'you'll have to come into my bedroom.'

Hélène's demure expression became a frown. I looked at my watch. I was in no hurry. I began to laugh.

'He doesn't mean his *own* bust,' I explained. 'He means one he bought in the flea market. Isn't that right?'

'Yes,' he said. 'At the porte de Vanves, down the road.'

'And will you show it to my secretary?' I asked.

'With pleasure.'

It loomed imposingly in a dark back room cluttered with magic lanterns and turn-of-the-century bronzes. It was one of those dummies they use in lingerie store windows to display brassières. But someone with a fantastic imagination had transformed it into a most extraordinary poetic invention. A wonder washed up on the shores of reality. The torso of a mermaid, the figurehead of some phantom ship. And the limbless body, arched as if still offering itself to the sacrificial knife, was smothered from neck to waist with sea-shells of every kind and colour, like petrified but still swarming kisses.

It was the most striking Surrealist creation I'd ever seen.

'What do you think of the bouillabaisse?' I asked Hélène.

'Very unusual,' she said.

'The man I bought it from claimed he'd found it just like that on the beach,' said Jakowski. 'He wanted me to believe it was a natural object. I asked him what he took me for, and he brought the price down.'

'Well,' I said, 'unless anyone's going to do a strip-tease or a flame-throwing act, we'll be getting along.'

We left. Poetry's all very well, but it doesn't butter any parsnips. I had more serious things to think about.

# 9 *Villa des Camélias*

We walked back to the car along the villa des Camélias. The Courtenay house looked as empty as before. I didn't know what my next step should be. If everyone involved in the affair started disappearing, I had my work cut out. I could only hope, among plenty of other aspirations, that the painter and his wife weren't away for long.

We picked up the car and made, via the rue Raymond Losserand and the rue d'Alésia, for the busy Avenue d'Orléans.* The left side of the street was packed with people moving about between the shops and the market stalls. The other pavement was less crowded.

I parked in front of the café *L'Oriental*, and we sat at an outside table overlooking the entrance to the Catacombs and the Belfort Lion in the middle of the square. After a while Hélène asked if I needed her any more, and when I said I didn't she left. I waited until the Ligne de Sceaux station clock said seven, then went inside the café to call Monsieur Armand Gaudebert. It's easier to lie over the telephone.

'I've been hanging around the post office all day,' I said. 'I needn't have bothered. No one by the name of Ferrand has come to collect anything from the poste restante. Perhaps something happened to prevent him. Maybe he's been arrested. For some other reason. Do you want me to check?'

*Now Avenue du Général Leclerc.

'Wait a bit longer,' he said. 'Can you keep watch again tomorrow?'

'Of course,' I said.

'If nothing happens then, it'll mean he's realized how foolish he's been, and given up. It'll show he was just trying it on, as I thought.'

'Probably,' I said. 'Good night, monsieur.'

He had no need to worry. Nothing would happen tomorrow either. The man with the tattoo wouldn't trouble him any more. But I'd no intention of telling him so. First because it was my secret. Second because the Gaudebert business had nothing to do with Ferrand's death. And third because it would be tantamount to admitting I was of no further use to him, and I didn't like the idea of having to repay at least part of his advance.

I stayed on at *L'Oriental* and had dinner in the brasserie. Then I went and sat out in the place Victor-Basch in front of the *Cyrano*, which has a notice saying it specializes in Bergerac wines. When it was quite dark I set off again for the villa des Camélias. Might as well see whether the Courtenays were back in residence.

I left the car in the rue Brune and walked the rest of the way. The air was full of the scent of privet and syringa, and everything was asleep. Or almost. Nothing seemed to have changed at the painter's house. There was no light either in the large windows of the studio or in the smaller ones of the house itself. So if I wanted an interview with Courtenay or with his incandescent wife I was going to have to wait. And I was going to have to get in the queue. Someone was there before me.

A darker shadow in the shade of a tree growing on the railway bank, he stood close against the fence, apparently watching the house. Then I noticed that one of the two windows at the front was open. I thought of the Rats of

Montsouris: perhaps the man was keeping watch while his mates were at work inside.

But I must have been wrong, because he didn't give the alarm when he realized I was there. Or if he did, it was only to himself. He left the fence and headed for the footbridge – not fast, but ready to break into a run if necessary. The light at the end of the bridge fell on him as he passed, but all I could see was that he was wearing a hat and was about my build. Like a lot of Parisians. I followed him across the bridge and then down the rue des Arbustes. At this point I called out to him, and he took to his heels and disappeared down the rue de Vanves.

He was a bit too fast for me, and I turned back towards the villa des Camélias.

From the middle of the bridge I could see light in the windows that had been dark before. Then it suddenly went out.

I took up the same position as the man I'd scared off, and stood watching the house. I wasn't sure what to do next.

Someone decided for me.

I heard a door open quietly, then the crunch of gravel and the sound of a gate opening. A man crossed the street and was in front of me before I knew what was happening. The scent of privet and syringa were replaced by the reek of gin.

'Might as well get it over with,' he whispered. 'Come inside. I want to have a talk.'

'I'd prefer to talk to your wife,' I said. 'But I suppose you'll do.'

I followed him into the house.

He put the light on in the hall; a picture on the wall caught my eye. We went upstairs. He switched the light on there too, then led me into a room where there were two more pictures. All three were portraits of the redhead;

starkers in one, naked in the second, and without a stitch on in the third. I concluded from this exhibition that my host used his wife as a model, if not exactly a model of virtue.

He was a short man, with big shoulders and feet, dull eyes, a toothbrush moustache and a distinguished head of salt-and-pepper hair. He wore an extremely worried expression and an expensive summer suit.

'You ought to take that revolver out of your pocket,' I said. 'It's spoiling the sit of your jacket.'

# 10 A hundred-franc clue

'The devil knows why I brought it,' he growled. 'I don't intend to argue. How much?'

'Let's sit down,' I said. 'This could take time.'

'On the contrary,' he said. 'It'll take no time at all. You've been prowling about outside long enough. We've both wasted enough energy already.'

I took no notice of this and sank into a comfortable armchair. I wasn't afraid of his revolver. I was more sorry for him than anything. He was scared enough for both of us.

'Isn't Madame Courtenay here?' I asked.

'Never you mind,' he said.

'I hope you haven't killed her,' I said.

'Never you mind,' he repeated. 'How much?'

'How much?' I laughed. 'I thought you didn't give in to blackmail. I understood you beat up anyone who tried it. Why the change of policy?'

'I don't know what you mean,' he said.

I pointed to the painting on the wall facing me.

'This time Messalina's done something even more stupid than usual, hasn't she?'

'I don't know what you mean.'

' "How much?" ' I said. ' "Never you mind." "I don't know what you mean." You haven't got a very wide range, have you? What about the fact that she was covered with blood? Do you know what that means, M. Courtenay? She's not just a cat on heat now – she's a murderess. Quite a different kettle of fish. That must be why you're in such a panic you don't even ask prowlers what they're up to. You just say "How much?" The only sum that interests me, monsieur, is a few million.'

'You're too greedy,' he said. 'I haven't got that much.'

'But the case I'm concerned with is on that scale. According to a lead I've been given. But of course it may be nothing to do with you. Unless this document—'

I took out the drawing and handed it to him.

'What is this filth?' he spluttered.

'A woman with no clothes on,' I said. 'Like your wife in those pictures. But this time she's with a gentleman. You wouldn't be responsible for this ribald little masterpiece, would you? I've been told by connoisseurs that it's very expertly done.'

'Maybe it is. But it's disgusting all the same. And nothing whatsoever to do with me.'

'Just as well,' I said. 'You've got plenty of other things to worry about. Right. Now it's time to put our cards on the table.'

I took the drawing back and put it in my pocket.

'Card being the operative word,' I added, giving him mine.

He studied it.

'Hm,' he said. 'A private detective. Who put you on to this case?'

'I'm old enough to put myself on to it,' I answered. 'Don't bother to work it out. Just tell me where your wife is. Remember, she's killed a man.'

He shook his head.

'That's not true,' he said.

'You don't say it with much conviction.'

He shrugged despondently.

'She's not responsible for her actions,' he said.

'You think she's guilty, then?'

'I don't know any more, ' he groaned.

'You love her,' I said. 'In spite of the way she's behaved and all the harm she's done you, personally and socially, you love her. It shows in these paintings. They're voluptuous, tender. Not cold and academic, as I'm told your "official" work is.'

'What the hell do you care whether I love her or not?' he growled. 'You're just a cop. You wouldn't understand.'

'I may be a cop,' I said, 'but I'm a private cop. That means I'm different. And I'm different from other private cops, too. Love, monsieur, passionate love, is something I respect.'

He looked astonished.

'Why are you telling me this?' he said.

'So that we can stop beating about the bush,' I said. 'So that you won't put my back up any more by offering me money. And so that you'll understand once and for all that I must see your wife, whether she's killed someone or not. Because I've an idea that she alone can give me some clues about a case involving several million francs.'

'So you respect money, too, do you?' he sneered.

'No, monsieur,' I said. 'I despise it. That's why I'm always broke. But as I'm always broke I always need it. It's a vicious circle. Very vicious. Be that as it may, the other night your wife was in a run-down tenement where a crime was committed. I was there myself, though I'd prefer it if no one else were to know. You're not the only one with secrets! I'm sure we can come to an understanding.'

I told him all I thought he needed to know, then said:

'I must ask your wife some questions. I swear I won't give her away. Where is she? In the country?'

'Yes,' he said.

'Not in a psychiatric clinic?'

'No,' he said. 'I've got a place at Saint-Rémy in the Chevreuse valley. We tried a clinic once, but it was no good.'

'I know. Did you take her out to the country today?'

'Yes. First thing this morning. I thought a bit of rest might . . . There's a local couple who've known her since she was a child. They're looking after her. I've never seen her come home in such a state from one of her . . . escapades.'

'Quite,' I said. 'They haven't all ended so tragically. What did she say?'

'Not much,' he answered. 'She was in a state of shock. She talked about a dead man. And she was wearing filthy old clothes, all covered in blood.'

'Which you threw on to the railway line.'

'Yes,' he said. 'There was an embarrassing incident before, at a dance in the rue Pernety. But that wasn't so serious.'

'Monsieur Courtenay, I must see your wife,' I repeated.

He wrung his hands.

'Give her a bit of rest,' he said. 'I assure you she's in no condition to answer questions.'

I couldn't force him to take me to her right away. I gave in. I could use the time to think, if I was still up to it.

'Arrange for me to see her as soon as possible,' I said. 'You have my card and telephone number.'

I stood up.

'One more thing,' I added. 'I'm as good as proposing to work for you, to help you out of your difficulties, for nothing. But there's one thing you can do for me. If any other member of the blackmailers' guild comes to see you, don't just offer him money, as you did me. Let him do the talking. Try to find out his name and address. Even if they're false they could be helpful. Can I count on you?'

He said I could.

I though he gave me a strange look as I left. He couldn't get over what I'd said about love and money.

I went home and tried to piece things together. It wasn't easy.

Ferrand had tried to involve me in an affair worth several million francs. He could turn to someone like me because, according to him, there was nothing crooked about it. This in itself was curious, given his dubious morals, but it might be true. The affair was apparently quite unconnected with his attempt to blackmail Gaudebert, the former public prosecutor. That had just been something on the side. Cigarette money. But if the redhead had killed Ferrand, mightn't *she* have something to do with the more important business? I began to regret having been so frank with her husband.

After ruminating about this and a lot of other things, I picked up the telephone. It was late, but the Fiat Lux Agency prides itself on functioning all round the clock.

First I woke up Hélène.

After telling her about my evening, I said:

'I'm still terribly in the dark, sweetie. But we must do something, if only to make a good impression. I've been wondering whether Ferrand didn't get on to the grandiose affair he suggested to me during his burgling activities. While he was working with the Rats of Montsouris. So tomorrow I'd like you to go and consult the back numbers of the *Crépuscule* and make a list of all the people in the area who've been burgled. That might tell us something.'

'All right. But it'll be the dickens of a job,' she said. 'For you, I mean, when you have to go round trying to drag information out of them all.'

I didn't need telling. And despite all our efforts we might be on a wild-goose chase.

'Make the list all the same,' I insisted.

'What ever you say, boss,' she answered. 'But I've been

thinking too, even if I have taken my time. Marie Courtenay may have killed Ferrand, but she certainly didn't remove his body. She was running away when you collided on the stairs.'

'She must have had accomplices,' I said.

'Are you sure?'

'I'm assuming it.'

'Something else has just struck me,' she said. 'It's not exactly an idea – more something I'd *like* to happen. You admit yourself you're in the dark, and it seems to me that unless something unexpected happens you're going to stay there a long time. The police have more means at their disposal than you. If they were to find Ferrand's body, they might open things up, and you could follow their progress, without showing your hand, by keeping in touch with Commissaire Faroux. And with what you know already, you could crack the case first!'

'It's certainly an idea, angel!'

'Just something I'd like to happen.'

'It's an excellent idea,' I said. 'Finding the body might stir things up a bit. If the worst comes to the worst, I'll do it myself.'

'Do what?!'

'Find the body. Are you deaf?'

'My God! You mean you know—'

'By the railway, where it runs along by the rue Blottière. Under one of the coal-heaps near the house; no one goes there much, and they're not too solidly packed. Of course I could be wrong, but I see no other reason why there should have been coal dust on the stairs. You weren't to know, but it wasn't there the previous day. It could only have been brought in by the undertakers on the way back from the burial. Good night then, sweetie.'

I hung up, feeling rather pleased with myself. Then I called Roger Zavatter, another member of the Nestor gang.

'I'd like you to go on a hunting trip,' I said. 'Starting tomorrow. I need to know the financial position of two very respectable gentlemen. To find out if they're worth blackmailing.'

'Charming!' laughed Zavatter. 'Who are they?'

'Monsieur Armand Gaudebert, who lives in the rue du Douanier, and Monsieur Auguste Courtenay, villa des Camélias.'

Zavatter wrote it all down and hung up.

It was hot, so I had a little drink. Then I smoked a pipe. That gave me another thirst. So . . .

If that was the only way to clarify the situation, I thought, why shouldn't I make the police a present of Ferrand's body? But I'd have to go carefully, and not give them so much help they'd solve the mystery before I did. You never know with them. I decided to get rid of the clothes I'd worn the other night. I couldn't wear them any more, anyway. I got them out of their hiding place and started to go through the jacket and trouser pockets for any incriminating evidence. Then I began to laugh. At least old Ferrand had brought me in a bit of lolly. Not exactly the millions we'd been counting on, but a start. Not only had his attempt at blackmailing Gaudebert earned me a decent retainer, but there were the two hundred-franc notes I'd touched him for when I was pretending to be down and out.

They were by no means new. One of them had been used as a memo. It reminded me of a thousand-franc note I'd once had, with 'Love and kisses. See you soon' written on it (it had probably been treasured by its owner, who'd only parted with it when he was completely broke).

There was nothing like that written on the note Ferrand had given me. Just two groups of letters and figures: *ALE*

78–09, and *DEN* 35–10. The first was my own telephone number. The second must belong to another of Ferrand's acquaintances.

It was time to turn in.

As soon as I woke up next day I called Anatole Jakowski.

'I forgot to ask you something about Auguste Courtenay yesterday,' I said. 'His house hasn't been burgled recently, has it?'

'No. What do you suppose he's got that's worth stealing?'

'You told me he was rich.'

'Oh, I see!' he said. 'Sorry! Yes, he must have some cash and jewellery in the house. I didn't think of that. Professional bias. As a collector, the only thing *I* worry about is not any money I may have on the premises but my collection. And the only thing I think of in connection with a painter is his paintings. But I can't imagine anybody being such a moron as to steal Courtenay's daubs.'

'Quite,' I said. 'Of course there are his portraits of his wife, but as one can have the original for the asking . . . So he hasn't been burgled?'

'No. I'd have heard about it.'

I thanked him and hung up.

I looked at my watch, and went down to buy the papers. Still nothing about the rue Blottière, and nothing about Ferrand, who must still be lying peacefully under his pile of coal. For the moment he could stay there. He wasn't costing anyone anything.

I picked up the phone again and dialled DEN 35–10.

'Hallo,' said quite a pleasant female voice.

'Hallo,' I said. 'Is that Denfert 35–10?'

'Yes, monsieur.'

'Could you tell me whose number it is, please?'

'You mean you don't know?'

'No,' I said. 'I'm ringing up to find out.'

A little laugh, then:

'I'd better call the doctor.'

'I'm serious,' I said.

'So am I,' said the voice.

I heard the noise of the receiver being put down, and then some indistinct sounds. Finally the phone was picked up again.

'Hallo. What is it?' came a gruff voice. 'Who do you want to speak to?'

'I've no idea. Are you the doctor?' I said.

'Yes.'

'Doctor who?'

'Who are *you*, if you don't mind my asking?'

'Sorry,' I said. 'I'm Nestor Burma. I'm a private detective.'

'I'm Dr Dalaruc,' said the voice. 'What are you calling about?'

'Frankly,' I said. 'I haven't the faintest idea. I must have seen your number somewhere.'

'And you just thought you'd give me a call?'

'That's about it,' I said.

He laughed.

'On impulse?' he said.

'You could put it that way.'

'Are things going all right for you at the moment?'

'So-so.'

'You're not overdoing it?'

'A little, perhaps.'

'I see,' he said. He had the perfect bedside manner. Just

right for dealing with other people's troubles. 'You'd better come round and see me. I live at the corner of the boulevard Arago and the rue Denfert-Rochereau. I think we should have a chat.'

If I wasn't mistaken he was trying to make a fool of me.

'I don't know what we'd have to talk about,' I growled.

'Oh, I'll know,' he said. 'That's my job. I'm a psychiatrist.'

And he hung up.

A psychiatrist! Well, that was a turn-up for the book. I thought for a moment. Ferrand had noted down two numbers. And as he'd attached some importance to mine, I assumed the other must also mean something to him. Perhaps he was consulting the doctor personally. No! Of course not! The image of Marie Courtenay, naked under her red dressing-gown, rose up before me. She'd been treated in a psychiatric clinic once.

I realized I still had the receiver in my hand and was sitting looking vaguely at it. I slowly put it back in its place. Since he'd invited me, I might as well go and have a chat with the shrink.

The sun blazed down on the place Denfert-Rochereau and the majestic green Lion of Belfort in the middle. The house I'd come to was on the corner of the boulevard Arago: a tall, respectable, five-storey building dating from the turn of the century. There was a chemist's shop on the ground floor. I'd be able to get some aspirins on the way out.

A pert little housemaid took my card, came back after a moment, and showed me in to Dr Jean Dalaruc. He was a man of about sixty, with a broad, furrowed brow and the chin of a martinet. His eyes were small and close together, and gleamed behind a pair of pince-nez that were constantly threatening to fall off. His obstetrician's hands toyed with my visiting card.

'So, you're Monsieur Nestor Burma,' he said. 'It was you who called me a little while ago. I thought it was a joke.'

'Not at all,' I said. 'You suggested I come and see you to have a chat. So here I am.'

He started to laugh, and his face was completely transformed. I could hardly believe it was the same man. Perhaps he'd learned the trick from one of his cases.

'You're a very obedient patient,' he said. 'Congratulations. And you really amused me just now. Do you mind if I look at you a bit more closely? . . . H'm . . . You don't seem particularly disturbed.'

'It's not for me to tell you that appearances are deceptive.'

'Indeed. And what can I do for you? If you wouldn't mind making it snappy. I have to go out and . . .'

He decided not to finish the sentence. Then, after putting my card on the mantelpiece among a collection of objects quite as bizarre as Jakowski's, and obviously the work of some of his patients, he came and stood in front of me with his head on one side. An attitude that almost proved fatal to the pince-nez.

'I'll be very brief,' I said. 'I've got just one question to ask you.'

He raised a hand.

'Just a moment,' he said. 'I've got one to ask you. How did you get hold of my telephone number? I haven't been in the phone book for a long time – I got fed up with being woken at two in the morning by practical jokers saying I must be mad to come to the phone at that hour. And you evidently didn't know whose number you were calling.'

'No, I didn't,' I said. 'And if you hadn't been a psychiatrist I might not have come to see you. But psychiatry fascinates me.'

'Yes, it's most intriguing,' he said. 'But how did you get hold of my number?'

'I found it in my pocket, on a piece of paper. Someone must have put it there.'

'To stimulate your imagination?'

'Something like that, I expect.'

'H'm . . . Let's hear your question.'

'It's about a crime,' I said.

'That's not a question,' he said. 'And it's more a matter for the police than for me.'

'Not just yet,' I said. 'Here's the question. Have you ever had a neurotic by the name of Marie Courtenay as a patient? A nymphomaniac, an alcoholic and a drug addict?'

'Is this an official inquiry?' he said.

'No.'

'Then I can't answer.'

'Professional secrecy?'

'If you like,' he said. 'Are you surprised?'

'Not in the least. I was expecting it.'

'In that case why did you ask?' he said.

'To see what you'd say,' I answered.

'And to draw your own conclusions?'

'Yes.'

'And what are they?'

'There aren't any,' I said. 'You're too clever.'

'Perhaps. But you seem to have the symptoms of a nice little case of interpretational disturbance. I'm only sorry I haven't got time to examine you.'

He looked at the clock. 'I'm due at Sainte-Anne's. Would you like to come too?'

'I may need a shower,' I said, 'but I prefer to give it to myself in a place where they cater for normal people. I'm sorry to have troubled you, doctor. You have my card. If you should happen—'

He interrupted.

'I fear I'll never be of any use to you,' he said.

I made my way to the door, but turned just as I was about to go out.

'The name of the man who put your number in my pocket is Ferrand,' I said.

'What about it?'

'I won't ask if you know him.'

'Just as well,' he smiled.

'How *can* people get hold of your number?'

'From my patients or their families. I don't give it to anyone else. And you must realize firstly, that my patients aren't keen to proclaim the fact I'm treating them. And secondly, that professional secrecy prevents me from giving you their names.'

'And thirdly, it wouldn't do me any good if you did,' I said. 'It would take me for ever to go through the list one by one. There's no shortage of crackpots these days.'

'No,' he said meaningly. 'There isn't.'

I left before he had time to get out the straitjacket.

Down in the street I cursed myself for an idiot. What had I hoped to get out of him? Was there anything to be got? Come on, Nestor! Perhaps you'll have more luck with the redhead. But I mustn't give her time to gather her wits too completely. I'd been a fool to let her husband get round me the day before.

I picked up the car and drove to the villa des Camélias. There was no sign of life in the painter's house. I rang at the front gate. No one answered. I began to sweat. Only one drop in two was due to the temperature.

'M. Courtenay isn't at home, monsieur,' said a voice behind me.

I turned to see a woman leaning her opulent and gelatinous bosom out of the window of a house opposite.

'Do you know where he is?' I asked.

'In the country, I expect,' she said, 'on a lovely day like this. I saw him go off in his car this morning.'

I decided I'd take advantage of the fine weather too.
I set off for the Chevreuse valley.
Something told me I'd better hurry.

I had hardly any clue to the whereabouts of Auguste Courtenay's place in Saint-Rémy-lès-Chevreuse, and I wasted a
long time trying to find it. But finally I drew up in front of
a sort of fake castle standing in extensive grounds.

The elderly servants – the local couple the painter had
told me about, who'd known Mary Magdalen since she was
a child – were too good to be true. Apparently people like
that are still quite common in those parts. I had the devil
of a job making them understand what I wanted, and then
understanding their answers. Finally I made out that yes,
Monsieur had brought the girl, that the girl had stayed on
in the house, that then Monsieur had come back and taken
the girl away and that neither Monsieur nor the girl was at
the house any more. Or, to put it in a nutshell, I'd come
all that way for nothing.

I drove back to Paris cursing. First at myself. Then at a
lorry I met coming the other way. Then at a Citroën I
overtook. And last of all at the sky. It had been too fine
for days. It couldn't last. It never does in the blasted Ile-
de-France! As I was going through Orsay the sun disappeared and it started to rain cats and dogs.

Paris was still dry. But it didn't have long to wait. Great
black clouds were moving slowly overheard, and such rays
of sunshine as did filter through were a nasty yellow colour.
The temperature had shot up several degrees. It was like
being in a Turkish bath. Some distant peals of thunder
heralded a storm.

I still went back to the villa des Camélias. I'd never heard
of this corner of Paris before, but I'd certainly know it
from now on.

But wherever the Courtenays had gone to, they hadn't gone home. I swore and left again. It was nearly time to go and turn in a progress report to Monsieur Gaudebert. I could easily go on 'watching' the post office indefinitely. It didn't involve much effort, and it could bring in a regular salary if I played my cards right and pretended it was a full-time occupation.

I drove along the boulevard Brune and the boulevard Jourdan to the *Babel*, a pleasant café opposite the Cité Universitaire where all races and nationalities fraternize under the aegis of Coca-Cola, pin-ball machines and juke-boxes. There I treated myself to a nice cold apéritif, then set off for the rue du Douanier, mopping my brow as I went.

# 12 Stormy weather

The ex-lawyer received me in the same office as on my first visit. The pretty little redhead with the golden-brown eyes was there too. She was wearing a different skirt, but the same clinging white top. Mouth-watering! And when I saw the two of them standing side by side, I felt quite frustrated. That's what psychiatry does for you!

'Ah! Monsieur Burma,' said Gaudebert, getting up. 'I think you've already met my wife. But I haven't introduced you formally. Henrietta, this is Monsieur Nestor Burma.'

Henrietta gave me her most gracious smile. We went through the usual polite exchanges and I looked discreetly at her hand. Perhaps her wedding ring made her finger too hot. She wasn't wearing it.

Gaudebert sat down at his desk again. Henrietta remained standing beside him.

'Right,' he said. 'So what's the situation?'

Drops of sweat stood out on his vast bald forehead, and the gaze that once made first the faces and then the heads of the accused fall, now betrayed a vague uneasiness.

'You can speak freely in front of my wife,' he added, seeing me hesitate. 'She knows all about it.'

'There's nothing new,' I said. 'Except that I'm starting to get some funny looks at the post office. Ferrand didn't turn up at the poste restante today either.'

Gaudebert frowned. The snarl twisting the corner of his mouth became more pronounced. He seemed to be listening to the thunder on the outskirts of the city. After a while he said deliberately:

'I don't like it. There's something strange about it.'

There was nothing strange about it at all, but I wasn't going to tell him that.

I smiled.

'No news is good news,' I said.

'I don't agree,' he said. 'I think it's strange that he hasn't shown up. What was the point of his ultimatum if he didn't mean to follow it up? I'm worried.'

I shrugged.

'He's an ex-convict,' I said. 'You told me that. I've already suggested that for one reason or another he might have been arrested. As I said before, I can check with the police if you like.'

Gaudebert didn't seem to be listening.

'I can't help wondering,' he said, 'whether he's hatching something – something I won't be able to do anything about. It isn't natural for a blackmailer not to keep an appointment with his victim.'

He was so worried he forgot I was there. His right hand reached across the desk and mechanically stroked his wife's hip. She started and grimaced, either out of modesty or for some other reason. But she soon controlled herself, and arrested her husband's hand by clasping it with her slender fingers. She looked out of the window. The wind had suddenly got up, swaying the trees in the Parc Montsouris. Gaudebert came to with a slight shudder, and withdrew his hand.

'I don't know what to think,' he said. 'All right. Go and see your friends in the police. We have to know, don't we? But be careful. Don't mention any names, will you?'

'You have my word,' I said.

I took out my handkerchief and mopped my face.

'Excuse me,' I said. 'It really is hot.'

He waved his hand vaguely.

'And if Ferrand *is* still at liberty,' I said, 'shall I keep on watching the post office?'

'What else can we do?' he said.

'Yes, I suppose you're right.'

He got up. His young wife stepped aside to let him pass. 'I'll see you out,' he said.

A flash of lightning forked across the sky, followed by a muffled clap of thunder.

'I'm afraid you're going to get soaked.'

As this wasn't meant as an invitation to dinner, I said I didn't mind, took leave of Gaudebert's wife and went downstairs with him. At the foot of the stairs I stopped and said in a low voice:

'If Ferrand isn't in prison I'll go on waiting for him at the post office, if you say so. But frankly, that's not going to get us anywhere. Now if I knew more about why he was trying to blackmail you— '

'Monsieur Burma,' he interrupted in tones of utter sincerity, 'I've already told you. I haven't the least idea.'

I left him.

Outside, a few large drops of rain had fallen like stars on the pavement in the rue Nansouty, which still stretched into the distance as thin and dry as a rake.

If Ferrand's name hadn't been mentioned in the note Gaudebert had shown me a couple of days before, made up of bits out of a newspaper, I wouldn't have had far to look for its author: Henrietta couldn't have loved the old man, and must have set up this whole business to make his life a misery.

There was a mirror over the umbrella stand in the hall. It had been put there for people to check their own appearance, not to spy on others. But it was hung in such a way as to reflect the stairs and the first floor landing, and as I came down I'd seen Henrietta come out of the study and stand with her hands clutching the oak banister. Her face, lit by a ray of light from a narrow window, was so hard it was almost unrecognizable. She was staring down at her so-called husband with a mixture of hatred and satisfaction.

Of course I might have been wide of the mark. Perhaps there was something wrong with the mirror. Then there was the stormy weather. A lot of women, and even men, are sensitive to atmospheric conditions. Storms set their nerves on edge. Alter their personalities. Still, if the message hadn't actually mentioned Ferrand's name . . .

# 13 Justice is satisfied

The storm came to nothing, like a project for tax reform. The first drops, which I'd seen in the rue Nansouty, were the last, and the rain-gauge in the Parc Montsouris – the best feature of the Bardo Palace, erected there after the 1867 exhibition – had to wait to quench its thirst. Leaden clouds still hung over Paris, anticipating the night. Only an occasional flash of lightning lit up the gloom, followed by a distant rumble of thunder.

I had a snack at the *Babel*, then made my way towards the villa des Camélias, just for a change. This time Auguste Courtenay was at home, and hastened to answer the bell. I don't know whether the government had cancelled a commission, or if he'd been asked to paint like Picasso from now on, but he looked very peculiar.

'Ah, Burma!' he exclaimed. 'I'm so glad to see you! Please come in.'

I followed him into the house.

'I was just trying to get you on the phone,' he said. 'My wife has disappeared.'

I frowned.

'I've had enough of this hide-and-seek,' I said. 'I'm too old for it. I come here: nobody. I rush off to Saint-Rémy: not a soul. I come back here: nix. I come back yet again and . . . I've wasted enough time already. Where is she?'

'I just told you – she's disappeared,' he said mournfully.

'Gone off on the razzle again?'

'Call it what you like. She must have left her room some time ago.'

Damn it! He didn't seem to be bluffing.

'Where could she have gone?' I said.

'How do I know? How can I tell where she goes every time she leaves the house?'

I took out my pipe to keep myself in countenance. But I suddenly felt hung over, and I knew smoking would make it worse.

'Tell me what's happened,' I said.

'There isn't much to tell.'

'Tell me what you did today – everything.'

He did so in a series of staccato sentences, full of repetitions and digressions. This is what it came down to: he'd decided to trust me, and to bring his wife back to Paris as soon as possible, so that she could talk to me and we could get the business over and done with. He'd driven out to Saint-Rémy first thing in the morning, they'd spent part of the day there, then driven at a leisurely pace back to Paris. Marie seemed better, but she was still tired and nervous, and when they got home the painter decided it would be better to wait a bit longer before informing me of her return. She'd gone up to rest in her room.

'I went up to my studio,' he said, 'and lost track of time. When I went to her room, she was gone! God! She hadn't touched a man for two days. It was obviously too much for her!'

'Perhaps,' I said. 'Did you tell her why you were bringing her back to Paris? Did you mention me?'

'Yes.'

'What did you say?'

'I tried to tell her I trusted you. I told her you wanted to question her about something that had nothing to do with her. That you weren't working for the police. And that even if she had done something wrong you weren't the kind of man to turn her in.'

'And how did she react?' I said.

'She seemed relieved, and agreed to meet you. And by the way, my wife didn't commit the murder. She told me how it happened. She was drunk and drugged to the eye-balls. She went out of her bedroom, I don't know what for and neither does she, and when she came back she lost her way and went into the wrong room. And there she fell over a corpse that was lying on the floor covered in blood. She remembers screaming, and then she ran away just as she was, half-naked and covered in blood herself.'

'It's quite possible,' I said. 'But why the devil has she run off again now, after agreeing to meet me and explain? I know running off is her speciality, but all the same . . . And how is it you didn't hear her go?'

'I've had my studio sound-proofed,' he said, 'so that I can work without being disturbed. And she must have left by an old service entrance. I found it open. Would you like to look at it?'

I shrugged.

'I'm not Sherlock Holmes,' I said. 'The position of her pillow and how far the door was ajar won't tell me the colour of her new boy-friend's hair. Assuming that she left for the usual reasons. I'm sorry to have to mention it, but she wasn't alone in that place the other night. She didn't tell you the name of that one night stand, did she?'

'I didn't ask any questions,' he said listlessly. 'I never do.'

We were silent for a moment. He paced back and forth in the darkening room like a bear in a cage. The sky was getting blacker and blacker. He switched on a standard lamp with an enormous yellow shade, and looked round as though he expected his wife to be attracted back by it.

There was a low rumble in the distance. Then it came again, closer and louder than before.

'It's going to rain,' Courtenay remarked, for want of anything better to say.

'Is that thunder?' I said.

'No,' he said. 'It's the train from the Citroën factory. It goes by on the old Circle line. When you can hear it that clearly it means rain.'

'You can certainly hear it now,' I said.

There'd been a loud screech on a whistle, followed by the din of buffers crashing against each other.

'There's been an accident,' I said.

We leaned out of the window, but we could see nothing from where we were. Then we heard steps running across the foot-bridge, and a man in blue overalls burst into the street. When he saw us he stopped.

'Have you got a phone?' he shouted. 'I want to call the police!'

'Come in!' Courtenay shouted, pointing to the gate.

A moment later the man was standing in front of us, sweat streaming down his face, which was pale under the grime.

'There's been an accident,' he panted. 'A woman jumped right in front of my engine. Oh, my God! Oh, my God!'

'Oh, my God!' I echoed.


She was barely recognizable, but there was no room for doubt. Marie Courtenay had adopted the horizontal position for the last time. But her beauty, which I'd been able to judge so fleetingly, could still excite interest. About a dozen shameless ghouls had gathered round her mutilated remains, doing their best to get an eyeful. The sort of people who appear from nowhere as soon as there's a gory accident. The kind that are regulars in the courts; that used to flock to public executions. Two cops had given up trying to move them on.

The accident had happened just inside the tunnel. According to the driver she must have been waiting in a kind of niche in the wall beside the track, and leapt out under the wheels. At least that's what he thought he'd seen. He was too shocked to say much.

'I didn't have time to stop!' he said. 'I didn't panic! It was just too late, for God's sake!'

We went and had a look at the niche.

It was a sizeable recess in the tunnel wall. The floor was covered with old bits of paper and straw.

'Tramps come and shelter here in the winter,' said one of the policemen. 'They get in through that hole up there. See? It comes out half-way down the bank. If they're drunk it's less dangerous than wandering along the track.'

'This wasn't a tramp,' I said.

'I've already told you to move on,' growled the copper.

'Not me, you haven't,' I said. 'I'm a witness. Nestor Burma. I'm with the victim's husband.'

'All right,' he said. 'But the rest of you, move along. I'll call in reinforcements otherwise!'

But the sightseers didn't budge until we went down on to the track again.

'It was too late!' the driver said again. 'There are plenty of other trains!' He pointed towards the main-line station at Montparnasse. 'And she has to go and choose mine, for God's sake!'

'Don't keep taking the name of the Lord in vain,' said the policeman. 'There's a dead body present.'

He was studying his tatty notebook as if reading from the script of a play.

'That's why I do it,' replied the driver. 'I don't normally swear.'

'Right. Where's your mate?' said the policeman.

'Gone to throw up.'

The copper pulled a face, and swallowed.

'We'll all be ill if we stay in here much longer. Let's move,' he said. 'She's not going to run away . . . Will you lot move along, for God's sake!'

He started to walk along the track, stumbling over the ballast as he went, and we all followed him out into the open air. The trees along the banks were rustling in a wind that seemed still to herald a storm. There were more onlookers on the foot-bridge, though at a more decent distance.

'Right,' said the copper, consulting his notebook again. 'The deceased is one Marie Courtenay, resident in the villa des Camélias, identified by her husband and by Monsieur Nestor Burma, private detective.'

He gave me a look.

'You're the first private eye I've ever seen,' he said. 'You were with the husband when—'

'When the driver came along looking for a phone and told us what had happened,' I said.

'And you came down here, and so on. Right. Are you a friend of the family?'

'Yes,' I said.

'Right.' He turned to the engine-driver. 'Have you informed your employer?'

'Yes,' said the driver. 'One of the bosses is on his way.'

'Right. Where's Monsieur Courtenay?'

'Gone home,' I said. 'And if you don't mind I'd like to join him.'

'I think that'll be all right. The Commissaire may want to talk to you, but for the moment I don't think . . . Wait a minute,' he said. 'What did you see?'

'Nothing at all,' I said.

'Just as I thought,' he said contemptuously. 'Private detectives!'

He searched his notebook for a line about private detectives.

'Luckily *we've* got people with a bit more savvy,' he said. 'Well, what is it, Ernest?'

He was talking to another uniformed policeman, who'd been left behind in the tunnel but who doubtless had plenty of savvy: he was on his way out with a piece of bloodstained paper in his hand.

'I found this in the pocket of her suit,' he said. 'Just listen! "Don't accuse anyone else of my death. I killed the man in the rue Blottière. I can't stand the shame." What do you think of that!'

'What does she mean – the man in the rue Blottière?' said the one with the notebook.

'I don't know,' said the other. 'We'd better go and see.'

'And better show a bit of savvy, too,' I said.

The first one gave me an old-fashioned look.

'What do you mean?' he said.

'Well, I don't know,' I said. 'You've got two dead bodies on your hands . . .'

'Not at all,' he sneered. 'If that's the best private detectives can do! Look, first she kills someone, then she commits suicide. That means . . .'

He consulted his notebook again, and this time I swear he read it off the page:

'Justice is satisfied.'

## 14 The body-finders

When I got back to Courtenay he was slumped in an armchair facing a picture of his wife, drowning his sorrows in a bottle of gin. Without standing on ceremony I took the tumbler from his hand and knocked back a good slug myself. He didn't protest. He just gave me a glassy stare and said:

'This is all your fault.'

'Don't be damned stupid,' I said. 'If you'd chained her to her bed—'

'That's against my principles,' he said.

'Mine too,' I said. 'Husbands who behave like that are pathetic bastards. But since you're not a bastard, you won't refuse to do something for her.'

'She's dead,' he said.

'She's going to be accused of a murder she didn't commit.'

'I know she didn't do it,' he said. 'But you said yourself—'

'Let me finish,' I said. 'I noticed a pond not far from your place in Saint-Rémy. The river Yvette is nearby. And isn't there a well in your garden?'

'Yes, there is.'

'And there must be a gun or two tucked away in some drawer,' I went on. 'You've certainly got one here in Paris.

Perhaps there's also a shot-gun in your collection, not to mention some rat poison in the loft and a lot of other lethal products scattered around. Am I right?'

'Well of course, in the country— ' he began.

'Wasn't she alone all day yesterday?'

'The Marchaux were with her.'

'The Marchaux? Oh, the country bumpkins! But they weren't watching her every single second?'

'No. Of course not.'

'She was free to come and go as she pleased?'

'Yes,' he said.

I laughèd.

'And with all those instruments of death to hand, and the time to use them, she came here, hid in a railway tunnel, and waited for that apology for a train to go by so she could throw herself underneath it?'

'Yes!' he growled, a dangerous light in his eye now. 'I see what you're getting at. Don't overtax your brain. Your argument might backfire on you. Yesterday she didn't know you were looking for her.'

'But you told me that came as a relief,' I said, 'that she trusted me!'

'Oh, I don't know any more!' he exclaimed.

He grabbed the gin again and drank straight from the bottle.

'Who looked after her before?' I said. 'I mean which psychiatrist?'

'Doctor Delanglade.'

'Delanglade or Dalaruc?' I said.

'Delanglade,' he said. 'Who's Dalaruc?'

'I've no idea,' I said, eyeing the gin bottle. But he'd drunk it dry.

'I think I'll go and have a look round,' I said.

'About time,' he belched.

He sent the gin bottle spinning across the room, got up, and went to the sideboard for another.

'That's it,' I said. 'Get blotto. But use the last remnants of your common sense and listen. You called me in because your wife came back in a sorry state the other night and you were afraid she'd got involved in some dirty work. But that's all you knew, OK?'

'Get the hell out of here!' he bellowed.

I left him with his litre of gin and went off to explore the bedroom. Nothing there. I traced the young woman's route out of the house and examined the lock on the old service entrance. It had been oiled recently from the outside, as if to prepare it for a pass-key or a picklock. A job that bore the marks of the Rats of Montsouris.

I went back to Courtenay. He was half asleep.

'You were right,' I said. 'She hadn't touched a man for forty-eight hours. It was more than she could stand.'

'Get out,' he growled.

I obeyed.

I got home just in time to avoid being drenched. The storm had finally decided to break. I took the telephone off the hook and went to bed. The rain pounded away dully all night. Like my brain.

I went to sleep late and woke up late. What with my involvement with Courtenay and the cop with the savvy knowing my name, I was up to the neck in trouble.

So I wasn't surprised that the telephone rang the moment I put it back on the hook. Nor to hear the dulcet tones of Commissaire Faroux as soon as I picked it up.

'Hallo, Nestor,' they said.

'Hallo, Florimond,' I replied.

'Were you expecting my call?'

'More or less.'

He laughed.

'In that case I hope you've prepared enough lies to keep me happy. You know how I love them.'

I thanked my lucky stars he was in such a good mood.

'Of course,' I said. 'There are plenty to choose from. You can pick out the best.'

'Thank you,' he said. 'Now, let's stop fooling around. It's too tiring. That storm hasn't done any good at all. The heat's as bad as ever . . . Now, let's see. Last night a woman . . .'

And he told me about Marie Courtenay's death as if I didn't know anything about it. Then, by way of conclusion, he added:

'You were at the scene.'

'Quite correct,' I said.

'Why?'

'Well,' I said, 'Madame Courtenay was a nymphomaniac, always out and about hunting for men. The other night, after one of her adventures, she returned home covered in blood. Her husband was worried. You know who he is, don't you?'

'Yes,' said Faroux.

'He lives in terror of her doing something really foolish on one of her escapades. Apparently it's already happened once or twice.'

'Once particularly – yes.'

'So to cut a long story short,' I said, 'he asks me to look into the matter. He sends the young lady to the country to calm down, and goes down later to bring her back to have a talk with me. When I turn up she's disappeared, and shortly afterwards . . . You know the rest.'

'Yes,' said Faroux.

I heard what sounded like the rustle of papers.

'Yes,' he said again. 'That fits. It's more or less what Courtenay told my colleagues. He was dead drunk, but he could still speak. Very good. You swear there's nothing else? I don't want you snarling things up.'

'I won't,' I said.

'Thank you,' he said.

I heaved a sigh of relief out of range of the phone. Then:

'As far as I'm concerned,' I said, 'the matter's closed. You take over from here. If there's anything to take over.'

'There is,' said Faroux.

'Oh, the note they found in her pocket,' I said. 'Saying she'd committed a murder. Had she?'

'It's not impossible,' said Faroux. 'She knew a man had had his throat cut in the rue Blottière. A crook called Ferrand. We *didn't* know, and we weren't the only ones. As soon as we told the Plaisance police about the note, they rushed to the street and arrived just in time to see the body being unearthed.'

'Unearthed?' I said.

'Uncoaled, if you prefer. He was buried under a heap of coal near the Montparnasse line. Some children were pinching the stuff—'

'Feeling the cold, were they?' I laughed.

'It won't be a hundred in the shade in the winter, will it?'

'True enough,' I said. 'So these children—?'

'Were stealing coal, and uncovered the body.'

'Which Mme Courtenay had stowed away there?' I said.

'Why not?' he said.

'Come off it. That coal's far too heavy for her to move!'

'So anyone would think from a distance,' said Faroux, 'but it's really shored up with a system of planks. Take one plank away and the whole thing collapses. At least, that's what it was like at the place where the body was found. A child could have done it.'

'According to you a child did do it.'

I'd have liked to ask some more questions, but it wouldn't have been wise.

'Well, so long, Faroux,' I said.

'So long, Burma,' he replied.

I hung up, went straight down to buy the papers, and read them over breakfast in a café.

They carried only a very brief account of Mme Courtenay's death. 'Suicide' was their word for it. There was no mention of the note.

They laid it on a bit thicker about Ferrand – especially my friend Covet in the *Crépuscule* – because of the mysterious circumstances surrounding the discovery of the corpse. The children who'd uncovered the body said it was an Arab who'd told them to dig in the coal heap. As soon as the dead man's shoe appeared, the man had taken advantage of the children's excitement to make himself scarce. Some of the papers said the children's story shouldn't be taken too seriously: a large colony of North African immigrants was gradually taking over the hotels, bars and corner shops in that area, and the locals tended to resent them and blame them for everything that went wrong. This attitude rubbed off on their children.

However, Ferrand, whose name wasn't known when his body was discovered, had been slashed to death with a razor. And, wrote Covet with great subtlety, from the razor to the Arab there's but a short step. Moreover, the children had said they knew this particular Arab: he lived in the rue Blottière, in the house next to the coal-heap. When the police searched the house, they found it had been taken over by squatters during the last few hours. The previous tenants had suddenly left.

The investigation was continuing, but with little hope of success. The Arab, if he had ever lived there, didn't live there any more. The owner of the house, who inhabited a much more desirable residence near the porte de Vanves,

The body-finders

hadn't been able to give any useful information; he'd sup-
plied a few names, but they didn't lead anywhere. A whole
series of people had moved into the ruin in the rue Blottière
and then out again as soon as they found something better.
Covet digressed on the subject of the housing shortage:
there were lots of houses like this in Paris, where perfectly
respectable citizens were breaking the law by living in
rooms passed on to them by friends, who themselves had
had them passed on to them by an official tenant whose
name still appeared on all the rent demands and receipts.

In short, it would be extremely difficult to trace the birds
who'd flown from the rue Blottière. You'd have to go back
through a whole network of relationships starting with the
victim. He had no name when he was found in the coal-
heap. There wasn't even a manufacturer's label on his
shabby clothes, or a single scrap of paper about his person.
But if there was nothing in his pockets there was something
on his hands. The police had taken his finger-prints, and
in less than no time they'd been checked with the records
at Headquarters and identified.

His name was Ferrand.

He had no Christian name. His parents had not only
neglected to give him one, but had themselves remained in
the strictest obscurity. No doubt by way of compensation
he'd 'worked' under the names of Courtois and Malbec at
various times in his adventurous existence. But he'd become
Ferrand again just before the war, when he teamed up with
a crook called Castellenot, known as a gentleman burglar
until he killed two men in the course of a break-in. Ferrand
wasn't involved, or at least nothing was proved. Five years
ago he himself was sent to prison, and he'd only been out
for a few months when he died.

I folded the papers, put them in my pocket, shoved my
minotaur's head in my mouth and went back upstairs. The
phone was ringing. It was Hélène, calling from the office.

'I was wondering what had become of you, boss,' she said.

'You do that a lot, sweetie,' I said.

'Is that a criticism?'

'Of course not, silly. Have you carried out those investigations?'

'Yes. And I've read this morning's papers. So they've found Ferrand. Was it you?'

'Careful what you say. The line may be bugged,' I said. 'Do I look like a North African?'

'True – you don't,' she said. 'What about Mme Courtenay?'

'I'd rather not tell you what she looks like. But you read about that too, didn't you? I'll explain all the ins and outs when we meet.'

'Come quickly, then,' she said.

'Not likely!' I said. 'I've already had a call from Florimond Faroux. If he finds out I was involved with Ferrand I'll never hear the end of it. He'll keep calling my place and the office, and he'll send round a couple of his junior officers. Not to mention Marc Covet.'

'He's called you three times already,' she said.

'See?' I said. 'I can't expect anything from those two but trouble. So I shan't be going home or coming to the agency. I'll have my office in the open air, either in the Parc Montsouris or outside a café. We must make the best of the fine weather – it won't last for ever. So come and join me at the *Babel* in the boulevard Jourdan, and bring the information you've collected with you. It's right next door to Gaudebert's house, but that doesn't matter. I don't need to kid him I'm on duty at the post office any more. He must have found out about Ferrand, like everyone else.'

I drove round to the *Babel*, where Hélène joined me in a dress I'd never seen her in before. Very snazzy.

## 15 The last burglary

It was peaceful but melancholy in the Parc Montsouris. We walked towards the lake under the lifeless gaze of the statues on the grass and the indifferent stare of the gardeners watering the flowers.

'I was as good as there when poor Marie Courtenay died,' I said as we went along. Then I told Hélène all about it.

'Was it suicide?' she asked.

'Yes, about as much as if she'd been found cut up in pieces!' I said. 'An awkward witness has been removed, Hélène, that's all. Marie didn't kill Ferrand. She wasn't even there when it happened. But maybe she talked too much and the murderer, or murderers rather, picked up her trail.'

'But how?'

'Oh, it must have been very easy,' I said. 'Marie rarely if ever knew who her lovers were. Perhaps a Christian name now and again. But *they* knew who *she* was. It's second nature to those blokes to go through women's handbags. And when she went off on the razzle she always took her bag with her. A woman rarely goes anywhere without a handbag. Except when she runs away starkers, terrified because she's fallen on top of a corpse that's not yet cold! And not only were there photographs in the bag she left behind in the rue Blottière – either she or the man, in a fit of sentimentality, had pinned one of them at the head of the bed – but there were also papers or something revealing her name and address. I caught a man keeping watch on Courtenay's house the other night. It's a pity he got away, otherwise Marie wouldn't be dead. He was waiting for the right moment to get in touch with the poor girl. But she wasn't there. Her husband had sent her to the country to rest. You could say what happened afterwards is partly my fault. Courtenay went off to get his wife and bring her back to meet me, and the man—'

I stopped.

'Yes?' she urged.

'From this point on I'm making a lot of guesses,' I said, 'but I'm sure it happened like this: the man comes back to the house again, sees there's no one there, and gets in through the old service entrance. Either to search the place – though I can't imagine what for – or to wait for the Courtenays to come home. If Marie returns alone it'll be a piece of cake. She does, or as good as. Her husband goes up to his studio and she goes to have a rest in her room. That's where the fellow's hiding, rightly thinking it's the most likely place to catch her alone.'

Hélène shook her head.

'But surely she'd have cried out when she saw him!'

'Perhaps she did,' I said. 'Even if only from surprise. But the man stifled her cries, and anyway Courtenay couldn't hear anything. As for Marie, she was a strange girl, and the man was an out-and-out bastard, I'm sure of that. But he was her latest lover. She still had the memory of him in her flesh. Courtenay expressed it neatly: "She hadn't touched a man for two days. It was too much for her." If you're too prim to understand, it doesn't matter. My point's still valid.'

'Men are real pigs,' she said, reddening.

'*I'm* not!' I protested.

'How do I know?' she said. 'So, anyway, he chats her up.'

'He gets her under his thumb once more and persuades her to leave home again. Then he takes her down on to the railway line which is deserted and easy to get at, and they hide in the cavity in the tunnel wall. It's from there she'll fall out in front of the engine. Everything's been worked out in advance down to the last detail. Whoever planned it all is either super-intelligent or completely barmy.'

'Sometimes it's the same thing,' she said. 'But I don't understand.'

I snapped my fingers.

'A hundred per cent barmy! That brings me back to the psychiatrists.'

'What psychiatrists?'

'Dalaruc,' I said. 'Dr Jean Dalaruc.'

I explained who he was and the strange way I'd met him. Then I went back to the tunnel.

'The man kills her in the recess. Strangles her, probably. It doesn't make any noise. Perhaps the only sounds came from Marie. Cooing "Darling, darling", thinking he wanted to stroke her throat.'

'Please!' said Hélène. 'Spare me the details.'

'You're right, sweetie,' I said. 'Especially as I wasn't there to see it . . . Well, once she's dead he waits till he hears the train coming, then pushes the body right under the wheels.'

'And how does he get away?' Hélène said.

'Either through the hole in the bank that the copper showed us, or more likely by mingling with the bloodthirsty ghouls who gathered round to gloat.'

'Either way you might have been a bit more on the ball,' she said.

'On the ball!' I said. 'Don't make me laugh. I thought it was a suicide myself at that point. Marie had never been a model of mental equilibrium, and she'd been traumatized by the events of the last few days. Suicide was a perfectly possible explanation.'

'And what made you change your mind?'

'The note,' I said.

'What note?'

'The papers don't mention it,' I said. 'It was in her jacket pocket. It said: "Don't blame anyone else for my death. I killed the man in the rue Blottière. I can't bear the shame." And it was something a cop said that made the penny drop. He said: "She killed someone and then committed suicide. Justice is satisfied." But people were too keen for that to be true. It made me think.'

Hélène made a face.

'So she didn't really write the note?'

'Certainly not,' I said.

'But they'll soon find that out.'

'The writing must be like hers,' I said. 'And they could put down any differences to her mental state—'

'You mean someone forged it?'

'Yes. Don't forget she left all her things behind in the rue Blottière, including the papers in her bag. It was all destroyed a long time ago, no doubt, but there must have been a sample of her handwriting there somewhere that could have been used as a model. I tell you, everything was planned in advance.'

'So,' she said, 'when you heard about the note—'

'It was the other cop saying "Justice is satisfied" that really made me twig. I said to myself: it won't be long now before they find Ferrand's body, if they haven't found it already. And I was right. By a strange coincidence an "Arab" gets some kids to dig around in a coal-heap and then, when they find the body, disappears.'

Appropriately enough, we'd just come to the pyramid erected in memory of the French expedition to North Africa who were massacred by the Touaregs in 1881. We sat down on a bench.

'But it doesn't make sense,' Hélène said, stroking her own thigh. (That way she could put a stop to it whenever she chose.) 'Some crooks killed Ferrand and hid him in a coal-heap. OK. He could have stayed there undisturbed for months. Even if Marie Courtenay had been a witness and needed eliminating, they could have arranged a "suicide" without bringing in Ferrand's body. I just don't understand.'

'It's devious but not illogical,' I said. 'They wanted "justice – i.e. the law – to be satisfied." To get shot of Ferrand's murder once and for all by pinning it on Marie Courtenay. Since she was dead, the case would be closed. The difference in social class between her and her "victim" wouldn't count in her favour – it would be accounted for by her being a nymphomaniac and more than a little cracked. And as for positive evidence against her – as Faroux pointed out on the phone, she knew someone had been killed in the rue Blottière, whereas the police didn't. And the body was well hidden. These facts don't exactly point to her innocence.

'And whoever's responsible is trying to pull the wool over *my* eyes too. They know I'm ferreting around without anything to go on, and they hope I'll swallow their version of the murder and suicide, and, with my witness dead, just let the whole thing drop. They hope Courtenay will make things easier for them by pulling strings and trying to hush up the story about his wife.'

Hélène started to laugh.

'So the whole thing was set up just to fool you!' she said. 'What modesty!'

'I don't know if *I*'m modest,' I said. 'But the amount of money involved in this little game certainly isn't. Ferrand talked about several million, and I'm growing more and more convinced he was right.'

'So who do *you* think is responsible for the killings?'

'The Rats,' I said. I gestured at the cool, silent, sweet-smelling park. 'The Rats of Montsouris.'

Hélène stifled an exclamation.

'That reminds me,' she said. 'I looked up those names you asked for, of the people who've been burgled.'

'And?'

'The gang's been keeping fairly quiet recently.'

'More important business to attend to,' I said.

'I just noted the names of their last three victims. One is a Monsieur Botrot, an old man of independent means who lives in the rue Beaunier. In the house where Lenin used to live.'

'I know the one. He also lived in the rue Marie-Rose – there's a plaque. Vladimir Illich moved around that area a lot before 1914. You too, it seems.'

'Well,' she said, 'as I had nothing else to do . . . I don't think M. Botrot's got any secrets worth millions.' She laughed. 'Apparently the thieves only took a few bottles out of his cellar. Oh yes, I forgot to tell you – it's cellars that the Rats seem to be chiefly interested in.'

'Is that so? . . . Go on.'

'There's an artist and engraver called Raymond Hillas who lives in the rue de la Tombe-Issoire, not far from the entrance to the Catacombs. He's got a terrible reputation. I caught a glimpse of him, and he looks shady too.'

'H'm,' I said. 'All that might mean absolutely nothing.'

Hélène looked me straight in the eye.

'Never mind the "might",' she said. 'It *does* mean absolutely nothing. The only thing that might be significant is this: the last burglary was at a villa you know quiet well. In the rue du Douanier. At M. Armand Gaudebert's house.'

A sparrow flew right under my nose and perched on top

of the pyramid. From there it took off again and fluttered up into a tall tree nearby. A single leaf floated down on to the gravel path.

When I'd recovered from my first stupefaction I took my pipe out of my mouth, stared at the bowl, then shook myself as if I had a whole flea circus under my shirt.

'That's shaken you,' said Hélène.

I shrugged and put my pipe back in.

'We're letting ourselves get carried away,' I said. 'Fantasizing. Dr Dalaruc could explain it better than I can. Gaudebert was burgled – OK. That can happen to anyone. It doesn't necessarily follow that that's where Ferrand got on the trail of the money. Even if it did happen on one of his nocturnal expeditions, which is by no means certain. And Ferrand wouldn't have tried to blackmail Gaudebert if there had been another way of getting at him. He knew perfectly well I'd never get involved in that game. The business he talked about, and which he said was straight, must have been something else. As for the blackmail . . .'

I told Hélène about the theory young Henriette's attitude had suggested to me.

'But of course,' I said, 'that doesn't hold up completely either, because the blackmail demand mentioned Ferrand's name.'

'Just a minute!' she said. 'You asked Zavatter to find out how well off Courtenay and Gaudebert are. Here's his report.'

She took some papers out of her bag and began to read aloud.

' "Auguste Courtenay: owns a house in—" '

'Don't bother with that,' I said. 'Courtenay doesn't interest me any more. Go on to Gaudebert.'

' "Armand Gaudebert",' she read. ' "Former public

prosecutor. Used to have a tidy fortune, but hasn't got a bean now" . . .'

I sighed.

'You see?' I said. 'We shan't find the millions in his house.'

' " . . . hasn't got a bean now because his so-called wife is so good at pouring money down the drain." '

'There's nothing unusual about that,' I said. 'It happens every day.'

'But what is unusual,' Hélène replied, 'is the young woman's name.'

I squinted across at the piece of paper. I had a feeling this was going to be a surprise. I decided to spare my heart by trying to anticipate it.

'Don't tell me she's Ferrand's daughter!'

'No, not Ferrand's daughter,' said Hélène, deliberately prolonging the agony. 'The daughter of a mate of his. Raoul Castellenot. A gangster who was executed for committing two murders.'

# 16 Crime of passion

I stood up. The bench felt like a bed of nails.

'Let's go and have a drink,' I said, pulling Hélène to her feet. 'Perhaps a snack as well. It'll soon be lunch-time, and we've nothing better to do.'

We went to the *Chalet du Parc*, a rustic sort of bistro inside the park that specializes in banquets and wedding breakfasts. It looks out over the lake, though sadly the latter has dwindled in recent years.

'Well, what do you think?' asked Hélène.

'Pretty spicy!' I said. 'A former prosecutor in bed with the daughter of a convicted murderer! Imagine what the artist who did the drawing in the rue Blottiére could make of *that*! My God, I hope they don't have any brats! I don't dare think what sort of outlook *they*'d have!'

'And what do you conclude from all this?' said Hélène.

'Nothing whatever,' I said. 'I shall see, as Louis XIV said. If there's anything *to* see. I'll go and drop in on Gaudebert by way of dessert. I've got to tell him Ferrand's dead, and so my post-office job's over.'

So I left Hélène to her coffee and made my way to the rue du Douanier.

The red-cheeked housemaid told me there was no one at home. Monsieur and Madame had gone out for a drive and wouldn't be back till the evening.

'Well, I'll come again later,' I said. 'Tell me, am I right in thinking the house has been burgled recently?'

'Yes, m'sieur.'

'When?' I said.

'A week ago Thursday, I think,' she said.

'And you weren't too frightened?'

'It was my day off, m'sieur. And I always spend that night with one of my friends from back home. Those crooks know everything, don't they?'

'Of course,' I said. 'And were Monsieur and Madame at home?'

'I don't think so, m'sieur. No, they can't have been there either.'

'Thank you,' I said. 'Tell Monsieur Gaudebert I'll call back this evening.'

I went back to Hélène and had a coffee with her.

'I can't get over it,' I said. 'The ideal couple! What a drawing that would make! . . . By the way, why don't we take a stroll to see that engraver who struck you as so shady? It'll calm my nerves.'

Little did I know.


He lived in the rue de la Tombe-Issoire almost at the corner of the rue du Douanier-Rousseau. The house had seen better days. The second floor had something of the look of an artist's studio, and according to the letter-box in the entrance that's where Monsieur Raymond Hillas lived. His visiting card was pinned on the door, and the sound of voices came from inside. When I knocked, the conversation stopped. I winked at Hélène. Perhaps we'd stumbled on something too.

'Come on!' I said, drumming on the door. 'Open up. We're not going to eat you. Is this the way you receive your customers?'

There was another short silence, then someone said:

'All right. I'm coming,' and a key could be heard turning in the lock.

'Come in,' said the voice.

I opened the door and we both went in.

A young man was sitting on a stool in front of a drawing board. He had thick lips and a big red nose, but didn't look any shadier than most. He did seem uncomfortable though, until he saw there was a woman with me. Then his face lit up.

'Come in,' he said. 'What can I do for you?'

Before I could answer, a second person came out from where he'd been hidden behind the door.

'I'm off,' he said. 'I'll be back, M'sieur Hillas.'

He was an Arab. Not badly dressed, but not well dressed either. Not too dubious-looking but not bursting with respectability. In short he was neither flesh nor fowl, and though I couldn't have said why, I didn't take to him. But dammit, there were plenty of other Arabs in Paris besides the one in the rue Blottière.

Crazy though it seemed, I couldn't stop myself.

'Easy does it, my friend,' I said. 'Don't run away so fast.'

'Must go, m'sieur. Sorry!'

He grinned nervously, showing yellow, pointed teeth, and tried to edge past.

I caught him by one wiry arm, but he pulled himself free and tried to run for it. When I tackled him, he pulled out a cutthroat razor. It was my turn to break free, so that I could get at my gun. Hélène shrieked, I sent the Arab flying through the door and out on to the landing, then went after him with my gun in my hand. Just to have a chat with him about the land where the orange-blossom grows. But I'd reckoned without Hélène. She'd flung the door to, and was standing with her back to it and her arms flung out.

'No, boss,' she gasped. 'Don't be a fool. He's a killer!'

'*The* killer, perhaps,' I growled. 'Get the hell out of the way!'

I grabbed her by the shoulders, shook her so hard I ruined her hair-do, and hurled her to the other side of the room. On the way she collided with Raymond Hillas, who had stood up and was looking on in amazement. The two of them fell spread-eagled on the floor. I left them to disentangle themselves and rushed in pursuit of my highly strung friend to tell him I knew of a good neurologist.

I spotted him loping along towards the rue du Père Corentin beside a fenced-in piece of waste ground. I was just about to sprint after him when a woman burst out of the waste lot behind him. I didn't get a look at her face; I just noticed she was rather poorly dressed. But I did see exactly what she was carrying. I opened my mouth to cry out, but it was too late. She called out to him and he turned round. Then went on turning, round and round like a human top, spun by the repeated whiplash of a .22 rifle. Then he collapsed face down, his body twitching spasmodically, and finally lay still.

When I bent over him he was dead.

I left him in the company of the professional gawpers and went back up to Raymond Hillas's place.

Hélène was waiting for me on the landing.

'Did he throw you out?' I said.

'No, I left of my own accord,' she said. 'I couldn't stay shut up with a man who does such horrible drawings.'

'They're not horrible,' I said. 'So it was him who did the one we found, was it?'

'A folder full of sketches burst open when I fell on top of him – thanks to your brutality, in case you'd forgotten.'

'Oh, stop complaining!' I said. 'You weren't the only one to get the treatment.'

'You've been at it again, have you?' she said. 'I heard some shots.'

'It was the Arab who copped it,' I said. 'Some woman filled him full of holes. A counter-terrorist, I expect. Is Hillas still there?'

'Yes.'

'Let's go in and have a chat with him,' I said.

'What the hell's going on?' he said when he saw us. 'This really is my day. Who are you, anyway?'

'Nestor Burma,' I said. 'Private detective. And don't try to play me for a sucker or you'll regret it. I want to know whether you do drawings like this.'

I produced the drawing from my pocket.

'My secretary tells me there's no doubt about it,' I said.

'That's one of the collection that was pinched when my cellar was burgled,' said Hillas. 'The bastards!'

'And that Arab,' I said. 'Did you know him?'

'Never saw him before in my life.'

'What did he want?'

'To blackmail me.'

I sighed.

'I've had enough of blackmailers,' I said.

'You're not the only one!'

'Do you often get visits from them?'

'No. That was the first, but it was quite enough.'

'Tell me about it,' I said.

He shrugged and his nose went from red to purple. The rest of his face was as white as chalk.

'What is there to tell?' he said. 'He turned up here and said: "I know the sort of thing you do." He didn't talk like that, but I'm putting it into more or less proper French. "I need a lot of those pretty pictures and some money." I was just going to hand over when you two turned up. My God, that was a real punch-up.'

He rubbed his wrist.

'I must have pulled a muscle when your dame fell on top of me.'

'You mean when I send the prettiest girl in Paris arse over tip into your arms, all you can do is complain?' I said.

'I don't give a monkey's about the prettiest girl in Paris!'

'Of course not,' said Hélène, furious. 'You've got your drawings. They must be quite enough for you.'

'Quite enough,' he said. Then, turning to me: 'Who was that Arab, for God's sake? He was pretty jumpy.'

'He's not quite so jumpy now,' I said. 'Did he want a lot of money?'

'Enough.'

'But you didn't exactly have a fortune to give him?'

'Of course not.'

'Didn't he give you the impression he was trying you out?' I said. 'To see whether he could make some other proposition, should the opportunity arise?'

He frowned.

'No. I mean, yes. Perhaps.'

'Forget it,' I said. 'I'm putting ideas into your head.'

'Yes, I think you are,' he said. 'Anyway, what could he have wanted, apart from the pretty pictures and a bit of lolly?'

'I don't know,' I said. 'But as you're an engraver . . .'

His nose went back to red again. He only needed the green to stand in for the traffic lights in the rue Vavin.

'Forged banknotes!' he said. 'That's an idea!'

'Don't say who suggested it to you when you come up for trial, that's all,' I said. 'Be seeing you, M'sieur Hillas.'

'The ship's sinking, Hélène,' I said as we went downstairs, 'and the rats are deserting and eating one another. But I'm damned if I know why.'

The police had removed the dead body from the street and taken it off to the cool shades of the morgue. Only a small brown stain on the pavement bore witness to what had happened, and gave the ghouls something to gloat over and the locals something to talk about over their apéritifs.

A troop of people had gathered outside the police station in the rue Sarette. We walked up and mingled with the crowd. We learned a good deal from their comments.

The woman tried to run away, but she'd soon been arrested and taken in. Her name was Molinier, Molinard, something like that. And the Arab's name was Muhammad. But then they're nearly all called Muhammad, aren't they? She shot him because he'd killed her other lover, a man named Ferrand. *He* was found with his throat cut yesterday, under a pile of coal in the rue Blottière. Well, I never! Did you ever hear of such a thing? But I thought Arabs were polygamous! . . . Yes, my dear, but they don't like the idea of women being polyandrous . . . Polyandrous? What will they think of next!

I pulled Hélène away. It didn't make things any easier if Ferrand had been the victim of a crime of passion.

# 17 A man's head

There was nothing to do but kill time. I invited Hélène to come and see a film in what must be the strangest cinema in Paris: the Denfert-Rochereau, in the place Denfert-Rochereau. It's underground and quite small, and you reach it via a narrow spiral staircase. The screen is small too, and is peculiar in that it's underneath the projection room: the picture is reflected on to the screen from a mirror at the other end of the auditorium.

When we came out I gave Hélène the evening off and went to Armand Gaudebert's place.

'Is Monsieur back?' I asked the apple-cheeked maid.

'He did come back, but he's gone out again,' she said. 'Madame's in, though.'

'Can she see me?'

She could.

Henriette was as pretty as ever, and there was a gleam in her slanting golden-brown eyes. Her auburn hair curled as if in protest against being cut so short. She wore a full grey pleated skirt and a blouse that left her sun-tanned shoulders bare. She was discreetly made up, with just enough lipstick to tempt any man who's normally endowed and doesn't scorn a bit of artifice.

Today I saw her through new eyes. It gave me a strange feeling to think her father had been guillotined.

'I came to report to M. Gaudebert,' I said. 'Or rather to give in my notice. You've seen the papers, I expect. That man Ferrand couldn't come and pick up the parcel at the post office because he was dead.'

'Yes, I saw,' she said in a soft, cool voice without a trace of emotion. 'Do sit down, M. Burma. M. Gaudebert will be back shortly. A cigarette?'

'If you don't mind I'll smoke my pipe,' I said.

'As you wish.'

She helped herself to a cigarette from a packet lying on a table. I lit it for her, waited until she had settled in an armchair, then sat down myself and took out my pipe.

'M. Gaudebert will feel safer now,' I said.

'Yes. I'm sure he will,' she said, arching her back and blowing a cloud of smoke up to the ceiling. Her eyes were sparkling and a smile of restrained glee hovered on her lips.

'You seem very happy,' I observed.

'My God,' she said with a little laugh. 'Is it as obvious as all that? Oh, well, why should I hide it? It's the weather. I love fine weather, don't you? Don't you respond to beautiful weather?'

She had tucked one leg underneath her, and her skirt had ridden temptingly high up the other one.

'Certainly,' I said. 'I respond to all kinds of beautiful things.'

'Monsieur Burma!' she cried gaily, 'That's naughty!'

She pulled her skirt down again. There was no hint of reproach in her voice. She was like a forward teenager.

'Beautiful things in general,' I went on, 'and ugly things, too. The death penalty, for example. I consider that a barbaric survival.'

Her lip trembled.

'Really?' she said. 'And why this profession of faith?'

'Forgive me,' I said, 'but my job's rather an unusual one. I ferret things out.'

Her face hardened slightly. She lowered her eyelids and looked up at me through long lashes. She seemed to be breathing faster.

'You . . . ferret things out?' she said.

'Yes,' I said. 'And I've found out that you used to be Mlle Henriette Castellenot. I don't think I need say any more.'

She burst out laughing.

'Ah! So you've found that out! It's not a secret, you know. Though some people think it is – blackmailers, for example. You wouldn't be a bit of a blackmailer, would you, Monsieur Burma?'

'No, I wouldn't,' I said.

'Just as well,' she said. 'M. Gaudebert and I prefer not to be reminded of that kind of thing, but we don't give in to blackmail.'

'There's are different kinds of blackmail,' I said. 'You can make a man's life a misery just by keeping a vague threat hanging over him.'

'It's you who's being vague, M. Burma.'

'Let me explain,' I said. 'I don't know when or how you and Gaudebert met and got involved with each other. Nor how long your happiness lasted. But I *am* sure that as things stand today you wouldn't be sorry to see him suffer.'

'And what makes you so sure of that?' she said.

'Certain expressions I've seen on your face when you don't know you're being watched.'

'You're mistaken.'

'And there's something else too,' I said. 'Ferrand.'

'Ah, yes! The blackmailer.'

'Yes,' I said. 'He was one of the Rats of Montsouris, the gang of thieves that operate in this district. They called on you recently, on your domestic's day off. M. Gaudebert certainly wasn't there, either. But you just might have been. You see what I mean?'

She shook her head mischievously. The happiness returned to her eyes. I must have been wide of the mark.

'No. Not at all,' she said.

'You were here when the burglars got in,' I said. 'You didn't try to stop them. You hid. But Ferrand was with them, and he found you. He was a mate and associate of your father's, and he recognized you. Or you recognized him. Anyway, you joined up again, and concocted the blackmail letter together. You hate Gaudebert: you and he are quite incompatible, and something like this was bound to happen.'

She shrugged her beautiful shoulders, got up and said shortly:

'Listen, M. Nestor Burma. I don't know if you're always this stupid, or if it's your idea of seduction. I know some women do fall for fools, but I'm not one of them, so forget it. I had nothing to do with that letter. I don't hate M. Gaudebert. Ferrand may have been an associate of my father's, but I was too young then to remember anything about it now. And the day we were burgled I wasn't in the house. As you like ferreting about, I'll supply you with all the information you need to check what I've told you. But now I'll leave you. You've got enough far-fetched ideas going round in your head to keep you occupied until M. Gaudebert gets back.'

She left me entirely alone except for a whiff of her perfume and the stub of her cigarette, smouldering in the ashtray. And my far-fetched ideas. I hadn't needed reminding of them. I was well aware they'd run away with me.

Time seemed to pass very slowly. Though in fact barely ten minutes had gone by when I heard one door open and another close. Or perhaps it was the same one. The maid came in. If I'd like to go with her, M. Gaudebert was waiting for me in his study.

'Hello, Burma,' he said with a thin smile. He didn't seem

in very good form today, either. He obviously hadn't had anyone's head cut off.

'I've come to say goodbye,' I said. 'I'm sure you've read the papers? So now we know why Ferrand never came to the post office. He didn't have the strength to heave the coal away.'

'Yes, I saw,' he said. 'Some crooks settling old scores, no doubt.'

'No doubt,' I said. 'Still, all's well that ends well. For you, I mean. Not for Ferrand.'

'Quite, quite.'

'You don't seem entirely convinced,' I said.

He seemed to come out of a dream.

'Me?' he said. 'Oh, I am, I am.'

He remained silent and thoughtful for a while, then said:

'All's well that ends well, eh? I wonder. Ferrand may have had . . . must have had accomplices, and if he talked about his plans—'

'Come now, monsieur,' I laughed. 'Don't let's shout before we're hurt.'

'Quite,' he said again, and the twist of his mouth became more pronounced. 'You're quite right . . . Tell me . . . Henriette – I always call her Henriette – says you know certain things.'

I raised my hand in protest.

'I've forgotten them,' I said. 'Apparently they're not secrets, but I'm treating them as if they were.'

'It's obviously the same thing that Ferrand found out,' he said. 'You see? His blackmail wouldn't have got him very far.'

I nodded.

'Nevertheless, there's something I'd like to explain to you, Burma,' he went on in a voice that was slightly husky. 'You must find it strange, indecent even, that a former public prosecutor . . . No, don't contradict! I know what everyone thinks. Everyone who hasn't been to prison, that is. Because, you see, at the Liberation – the Liberation! – I was sent to prison myself. And when I came out I was a changed man.'

He tried to clear his throat but only partially succeeded.

'Before, they called me the Chopping Judge, but prison blunted my appetite. I saw the world through different eyes. I knew that Raoul Castellenot – that gangster, that sewer rat, that executed murderer – had had a daughter. So I had her looked for. And I took care of her. There was no one else to. Then, one day . . . One wonderful day—'

His voice broke, then turned into a kind of sneer before he managed to bring it back under control.

'I was a widower. I had no children. I . . . She was more or less my adopted daughter. But she wasn't officially adopted . . .'

'And she's not officially your wife, either,' I said. 'Not to put too fine a point on it, she became your mistress?'

'Yes,' he said. 'I broke off all my professional and social contacts. I stopped seeing people of my own class – my own caste, if you prefer. All I had left was Henriette.'

He made a sweeping gesture, including everything. His chin quivered with emotion.

'I understand, monsieur,' I said.

He led me to the door of his study.

'Many people don't,' he said. 'People who talk about charity and redressing wrongs. I wanted to make up for what I'd done, Burma, by bringing up that little girl. But perhaps it was a mistake, seeing how it's turned out. Ah, well—'

'Make up for what you did?' I said. 'You mean her father . . .'

He nodded.

'Yes,' he said. 'It was because of me that he was sentenced to death.'

# 18 Beauty and the bust

I drove home and went to bed early.

Despite what Gaudebert had said, his situation provided a mouth-watering motive for blackmail. Henriette hadn't tried to hide it: neither of them liked to be reminded of the past. A crook might well hope to make a bit of money out of it. But not millions. Firstly because the secret wasn't all that scandalous, and secondly because, according to Zavatter, Henriette had already spent her husband's money. So I had to allow for the possibility that while burgling Gaudebert's house Ferrand had discovered the truth about the couple's weird relationship, and tried to make a little bit of cash out of it. But that meanwhile, in another part of the forest, he'd stumbled on something quite different and much more lucrative. And something that as far as he was concerned had come completely unstuck.

But I hadn't the faintest idea what it was!

Suzanne Molinier might have helped me, but Suzanne Molinier was in the clink. She was the woman who had used the Arab in the rue du Père-Corentin for target practice. The papers explained how she'd been Muhammad's mistress, how she'd dumped him to go off with Ferrand, and how Muhammad had sworn he'd kill Ferrand at the first opportunity. He must have kept his word, because Ferrand had been found with a closer shave than usual under a coal-heap. At first Suzanne hadn't been unduly worried by Ferrand's absence, but then she'd put two and two together and avenged his death, as well as certain other unspecified grievances.

I'd got thus far with the morning papers and my reflections on them when the telephone rang.

'Hallo,' said a jovial voice. 'Monsieur Nestor Burma? This is Jean Dalaruc, the psychiatrist. I don't know if you remember me?'

'We spoke only forty-eight hours ago,' I answered. 'I haven't lost my memory yet.'

'Nor have I,' he said. 'I enjoyed talking to you the other day. I like you.'

'So much the better. I think I'm going to need a few sessions of electric shock treatment. You might give me a discount.'

'With pleasure,' he said. 'But for the moment I'm calling because I may, without betraying any professional secrets, be able to help you in your investigations.'

'Yes?' I said.

'You mentioned a Mme Courtenay—'

'Whom you never treated,' I said. 'I've checked it out since.'

'That's correct. She's never been one of my patients.'

'And she isn't likely to be,' I said. 'She's dead.'

'What?'

'She's dead.'

He laughed.

'I must say there's a high mortality rate among the people you know.'

'Why do you say that?'

'You mentioned another name: Ferrand,' he said. 'I see

in the papers that he's dead too. And I also see that he used to be the friend of a certain Raoul Castellenot.'

It was my turn to laugh.

'He's dead as well,' I said. 'From a rush of blood from the head. It happened not far from where you live. At the Santé prison, one pale dawn.'

'That'd surprise me,' he said. 'I saw him only yesterday, and he was as right as rain.'

'What?'

'He's been in the Sainte-Anne mental hospital for about ten years. Out of his mind as a result of all that's happened to him.'

'I must see him, doc!' I shouted. 'I must see him!'

It burst out before I had time to think about it. It made no sense. What could I possibly gain by seeing him?

But I did see him.

He was sitting on the narrow bed in his small, bare room. He seemed to be living in another world, but no more insane than a lot of people who haven't been certified and who wander about freely. He must have been a strapping fellow once, but now he was like a stick. He had enormous golden-brown eyes with a strange gleam in them. He'd passed them on to his daughter. His elegant hands moved incessantly, as though the fingers were sifting sand.

'Did you find out anything?' said Dr Dalaruc when I decided I'd seen enough. He spoke ironically. He probably thought private eyes were all crazy.

'I'm not Sherlock Holmes,' I said. 'I don't know what on earth I expected to find out. He would have had to open his mouth to be of any use, anyway. Is he always that chatty?'

'He only talks to his daughter,' said Dalaruc. 'A very nice girl. She comes to see him regularly. I don't know if he recognizes her, but he talks to her. And he seems to love her deeply.'

'And what about her?' I said.

'She adores him. You can see it.'

I laughed.

'Crooks have very highly developed family feelings. It's a well-known fact. Hard head but tender heart, and loves his old mum, as they used to say in the army.'

'Oh, but *she*'s not a crook,' he said. 'She has quite a distinguished position in society.'

'I don't doubt it,' I said. 'So he only talks to his daughter?'

'Yes. Otherwise he writes. All the time. Poems of sorts, like a lot of mental patients. I plan to publish an anthology of their work one day. Castellenot's poems will be there. They're as good as any of the others, and what's more, he's an interesting character. You know what happened to him, don't you?'

'Not exactly,' I said. 'I only know he killed two men.'

Dr Dalaruc narrowed his little eyes.

'I can't tell you much about that,' he said. 'But he's made a sort of profession of being sentenced to death. Both the civil and the military authorities were after him. And yet here he is still alive. If you can call this living. But who knows? He may be happier than a lot of other people. Would you like to read some of the things he's written?'

The doctor had been kind enough to bring me here. The least I could do was admire the madman's elucubrations.

While we were walking to his office Dalaruc told me what he knew about his patient.

'Profession is the only word for it,' he said. 'He was sentenced to death in 1939, just before the war, for killing those two men, but he escaped while being transferred from one prison to another. Not a sign of him during the first part of the war, but the Germans got hold of him at the beginning of the Occupation. They arrested him, tortured him and condemned him to death – I don't know on what grounds. But instead of being executed he got away, or rather was kidnapped by some other Germans. But he escaped from them, too. Then he joined the Resistance. Let me make myself clear, Burma. I'm not trying to make out he's a saint. He's anything but that. I think he wanted to do business with both sides, and it worked out for a time but ended up in disaster. Anyway, the Germans caught him again, gave him the water treatment and beat him up, and then—'

'Sentenced him to death again?'

'No. To be deported. But his luck still didn't desert him. The train taking him from Compiègne was ambushed by the Resistance, and our friend took off again into the blue. After that, well, there are gaps in my information. All I know is that in August 1944 he was living in the Catacombs – they'd become the Resistance HQ. He behaved with outstanding bravery during the Liberation of Paris, but his mind had suffered as a result of all his experiences. And to make matters worse the police hadn't forgotten he was still under sentence of death. So they nabbed him. When they saw the state he was in they claimed he was shamming, but the facts finally had to be faced. He was mad. Incurably mad. And he's been with us for the last ten years. Just like a novel, isn't it?'

'Yes,' I said. 'And does he write about all his vicissitudes?'

'No. He writes mostly about women's breasts.'

'A mammary complex, perhaps.'

'You leave our vocabulary alone,' said the doctor. 'We have enough trouble knowing what we mean ourselves.'

In his office he took out a folder and handed me a few sheets of paper. I read:

For the beauty of the bust, the teeth of the oysters, the golden slime of the snails, the breasts devoured, digested, oh my sea-shore cadaver . . .

There were fifty or so lines in the same vein, and the same phrases kept recurring:

For the beauty of the bust with pearls on the breasts my trunk-woman my pearls more than pearls in the eyes the golden slime of snails the breasts have dug the sand the golden sand for the beauty of the bust . . .

I handed back the ex-gentleman-burglar's prose poetry and left the hospital. The rue Cabanis was sweltering in the sun.

For the beauty of the bust . . .

The words fitted Anatole Jakowski's astounding dummy like a brassière.

I spent the afternoon in the cool of the National Library, looking for articles about Raoul Castellenot and his exploits in dusty back numbers of the 1939 newspapers. I learned a number of interesting things: in particular that it had been more by accident than design that he'd killed the two night-watchmen during the break-in at the Lascève jewellery store. Still, they were dead just the same, and as they were model employees their corpses had weighed heavily in Castellenot's already bulky file and he'd been assigned the supreme penalty. During the robbery some enormously valuable pearls had disappeared; they were never found. Castellenot's friends were also mentioned. Not all of them were crooks. He was a gentleman burglar, a sort of minor Arsène Lupin and a friend of the arts. I thought of his present literary output. It showed the influence of those past acquaintances.

From the newspapers I moved on to a map of the quarries of Paris, concentrating on those that lie under the 14th arrondissement, which has been so burrowed into it's like a piece of Gruyère cheese. Finally I left the austere pile in the rue de Richelieu and went off to do some phoning.

First I called M. Grandier of the International Insurance Company, a gentleman who'd once been very satisfied with my services, and asked him to introduce me to someone high up in the hierarchy of one of his competitors, the Atlas-Albatross Agency.

'Try Loriot,' he said. 'He's an old friend of mine and he knows who you are. I mentioned you to him after you worked for me. Here's his number.'

'Hello, M. Loriot?' I said a few minutes later. 'This is Nestor Burma.'

I told him how I'd got his number and we exchanged the usual formalities, then I said:

'Did you ever find the Lascève pearls?'

'Alas, no.'

'Are you still offering the reward?'

'Yes,' he said. 'Have you found out something?'

'Perhaps.'

'I hope this is more genuine than the anonymous caller we had the other day.'

'Anonymous caller?' I said.

'Yes. A man who asked us the same question about the reward.'

'I assume he didn't ask for you personally?'

'No,' he said. 'But I spoke to him. It's still a matter of great concern to us, you understand. We can't neglect the smallest clue.'

'And this man didn't give his name.'

'No.'

'Did he have an accent?'

'No,' he said. 'No accent. But he did speak in a whisper.'

'Thank you very much, M. Loriot.'

Then I went to see Anatole Jakowski in the rue des Mariniers.

'I think,' I said without too much preamble, 'you had a
sixth sense the day you bought your famous snail and sea-
shell bust. Ever heard of Jeff Hariston? He was an expatri-
ate American living in Montparnasse in 1939, and according
to the papers at the time he was the friend of a gangster
named Castellenot. Hariston painted a bit, but chiefly he
made and collected poetic objects rather like yours.'

'That's right,' said Jakowski. 'I knew Jeff Hariston
slightly.'

'Mightn't your bust have come from his collection?'

'Anything's possible,' he said. 'Only he died during the
Occupation, and his "degenerate art" collection was dis-
persed. How could anyone tell if the bust had belonged to
him?'

'Didn't he make some kind of a mark on his pieces?'

'No.'

'Too bad,' I said. 'But listen to this — ' and I recited
part of the poem, 'For the beauty of the bust, the teeth of
the oysters . . .'

'Don't you see a connection between this and your bust?'
I said when I'd finished.

'Yes,' he said. 'They seem to go together. Who wrote
it?'

'A madman,' I said. 'Castellenot. He pinched a lot of
immensely valuable pearls in 1939 and they've never been
found. I reckon he hid them, in cahoots with Jeff Hariston,
inside one of the American's creations. In fact, inside your
bust. And it's the memory of all this that makes him keep
writing these poems in his little room. The same phrases
recur over and over again.'

'You mean . . . You mean . . .' Jakowski stuttered. 'And
how much would the pearls . . . ?'

'Several millions,' I said.

He gulped.

'Let's go and have a look.'

We went through into the room where the bust was on show. I saw it now in a new light: it seemed even more sensational.

'What do we do?' said my host, clearing his throat.

'It's yours, isn't it?' I said. 'I'll leave you to decide. But still, if I were you, I'd pull off a few shells here and there, just to see.'

We took off more than half – with great care, so we'd be able to stick them back on again. And all for nothing. It was true that the madman's poem couldn't have fitted this museum piece more neatly. But the Lascève pearls weren't there. That would have been too good to be true.

That evening Hélène and I had dinner together.

'That explains Ferrand's millions,' I said. 'He thought he was on the trail of the pearls. And as he couldn't take care of it all by himself, and didn't want his moth-eaten mates from the Rats of Montsouris to get anything out of it, he called me. If he went to the police the chances were he'd be in trouble. If he worked with me he'd have his part of the reward. And it really was straight.'

'Did he pick up the trail when he burgled Gaudebert's?' Hélène asked.

'Not the trail as such,' I said. 'But he found Henriette, if not in person at least in some documents – say some photos of her and her father. She loves her father very much, and she certainly has photos of him in her bedroom. I suppose it must have been a revelation to Ferrand. He hadn't heard of Castellenot for a long time and must have thought he was dead, then all of a sudden he finds his mate's daughter, along with proof that the father's alive too. He even found the psychiatrist's visiting card and took down the number. He must have thought it would be child's play to worm the truth out of the madman, find the pearls, give them back and pick up the reward – even if he didn't feel capable of doing it alone. He'd already called the insurance company to find out if the reward was still on offer when he died.'

'But why was he killed?' said Hélène.

'I think almost by accident,' I said. 'I've thought about it a lot. All his precautions came to nothing and his game was spotted by his colleagues in the Rats of Montsouris, who – That's funny . . . I'll tell you about something else later – who'd become suspicious and wanted to know what he was up to, without me getting a look at them. So, as soon as I left his place they sent a man round to see him. Now this bloke had sworn to get Ferrand because Ferrand had pinched his girl, so he took advantage of the opportunity to do him in. He could do so with a clear conscience because all he'd done was execute a traitor. The only thing is, this murder, this accident, must have sparked off a lot of other trouble.'

'What trouble?'

'I haven't got enough to go on, yet,' I said. 'Meanwhile the pearls haven't been found, they're not where I thought they were, and the reward still stands. Perhaps the beautiful Henriette will be able to dig back into her childhood memories and help me. I'll go and chat her up tomorrow and try to seem intelligent. She told me she doesn't like fools.'

Hélène gave an irritated shrug.

'What was the funny thing you were going to tell me about the Rats of Montsouris?'

'That their leader doesn't break into people's cellars simply to stock up on wine and liqueurs. He's looking for an entrance to the Catacombs; either one he knows about, or one he hopes exists. You remember the pot-holers Ralph Messac told us about the other day at Jakowski's? Well, they're all from the same gang.'

'Are you sure?'

'I'd swear to it,' I said.

Hélène frowned.

'But they must have been taken to the police station, mustn't they?'

'Certainly.'

'So, all we have to do to get their names is to—'

'Look at the day-book at the station in the rue Boyer-Barret. Yes, my love.'

'Are you going to pass this on to Commissaire Faroux?'

'Not for the moment. I prefer to leave myself room for manoeuvre. And if Marie Courtenay's killer is one of the pot-holers, the delay won't let him off any of what's coming to him, don't worry.'

'It's up to you,' said Hélène. 'But why are they so interested in the catacombs?'

'Because Castellenot lived down there for some time.'

'You mean—'

'They're looking for the pearls, too,' I said. 'Perhaps they burgled Gaudebert's place because they knew his wife was Castellenot's daughter and they were looking for some special clue.'

I burst out laughing.

'And there was poor old Ferrand, imagining he'd made a real find!'

# 19 Rat trap

Armand Gaudebert looked at me with surprise and suspicion. However he tried to conceal it, he must have lived in dread of blackmailers, and my visit made him anxious. To dispel any misunderstanding I said with a smile:

'I haven't come to ask you for money – I've come to offer you some. I have a business proposition to make to you. Forgive me, but my job is to ferret things out, and I just can't stop myself. And, to come to the point, I know you're not very well off, so I've brought you a few million francs. Excuse such plain speaking.'

When I mentioned his finances he gave me a severe who-on-earth-do-you-take-yourself-for-mind-your-own-damn-business kind of stare. But at 'a few million francs' he started.

'A few what?'

'Millions,' I said.

He shook his head in disbelief.

'I don't understand,' he said. 'Why don't you keep them for yourself, if they really exist? Why do you want me to have the benefit of them?'

'I'll be frank,' I said. 'I don't belong to the Society for the Protection of Retired Lawyers. I need your help. Or rather, your wife's.'

'I don't understand,' he said again.

'Let's call a spade a spade, shall we? Neither of us likes mincing words. You know that Henriette's father – your father-in-law, to all intents and purposes – stole the Lascève pearls in 1939, that two men were killed in the process, and that you, as public prosecutor, conducted the case against him and called for the death penalty. But for once the sentence, though passed, was not carried out – which was just as well for you, as it makes your situation vis-à-vis your wife less painful. After a whole series of adventures which I won't go into for the moment, Castellenot went mad and now he's a patient at Sainte-Anne's.'

'I know all that,' said Gaudebert.

'You must also know that the pearls have never been found. Castellenot made a good job of hiding them.'

He seemed interested.

'You haven't found them by any chance?'

'No,' I said. 'But what I'm suggesting is that you lead me to them.'

'You're too late, Burma. We've looked for them too, and found nothing. I should have liked to return them to their owners, both for Henriette's and for her father's sake. It would have completed his rehabilitation. But we couldn't find them.'

'I may have information you lacked,' I said. 'I ferret things out, as I said before.'

He didn't answer. Instead he turned away and gazed through the window at the trees in the Parc Montsouris. Beads of sweat stood out on his billiard-ball brow.

'What information?' he said at last.

He was talking to the trees rather than to me, and I took advantage of this to give him only a vague answer.

'I want you to ask Mme Gaudebert if she'll allow me to go ahead with these investigations. I'd like her to sift back through her childhood memories for me – for us. What she might see as a quite unimportant detail could open up new possibilities for me, in the light of what I already know.'

He shifted in his chair and adopted a patronizing tone.

'What are you after, Burma?' he said. 'You don't intend to run off with the swag yourself, I hope. Using me as an accomplice!'

'There is a reward,' I said.

He smoothed his bushy eye-brows.

'True,' he said.

He got up slowly.

'One moment, please. I'll go and ask her.'

He went out, and returned shortly afterwards with Henriette. She'd agreed to my request. She was smiling, and her eyes had all their old sparkle. She didn't seem to be holding what I'd said the other day against me.

'I'm minding other people's business again!' I said as we shook hands.

'Not at all,' she said amiably. 'We're delighted with your suggestion, and hope you'll succeed. If the pearls are returned it will make up for a little of what happened in the past. And if I can help—'

She couldn't, much. She'd been very young when the unfortunate affair took place, and even if she'd noticed anything at the time she'd forgotten it by now. When she spoke about her father, which she did at length and in tones of genuine emotion, she was a different person – a strange mixture of someone more mature than the young woman I knew and a very small girl. I gleaned nothing from all she said about his tastes and habits, nor from what she told me of her conversations with him at the hospital. I did my surrealist poet act and recited the piece about the beauty of the bust – I *had* been told I'd have a great future in the theatre – then told her about the strange object itself and my failure to find the pearls in it. But nothing rang a bell with Henriette. When I left the house we'd made no progress at all.

Night was casting stealthy shadows along the avenue Reille. The sinister bulk of the Montsouris Reservoir rose up in front of me. Plenty to drink in there. At least two hundred million litres. Two hundred thousand cubic metres kept in a maze of stone underground vaults supported by pillars reaching deep down into the smooth cold water. At the entrance to the lower reservoir – the larger and deeper of the two – there's an aquarium full of trout, tiny civil servants working in silence day and night to bear witness to the purity of the water.

I went home to bed, but it took me a long time to get to sleep. I knew I was asleep when I saw Raoul Castellenot in the bedroom, red with his victims' blood, together with Armand Gaudebert in his prosecutor's gown and wig, and Henriette with nothing on at all except Marie Courtenay's red dressing-gown and a widow's veil, also red, over her beautiful auburn hair.

She was laughing.

'This time I think I'm on to something,' I said.

Henriette shot me a golden-brown glance and Gaudebert tilted his heavy head to one side.

'Really?' he said.

'Yes. The pearl's hiding-place has been changed several times. Castellenot wasn't as mad as all that. One of the caches was the bust I told you about yesterday. The poems he writes have hidden meanings, and I'm sure my interpretation of the one I quoted was correct. But the pearls aren't there any more, so we can forget about it. Instead, let's try to see where Castellenot could have hidden them last. Where did he spend the last part of his life as a free man, physically and mentally? Answer: in this part of the city. Or rather, under it. In the Catacombs. That's why – ' I took out my handkerchief and mopped my brow ' – the burglars known as the Rats of Montsouris have been going though this area, breaking mostly into cellars and basements.'

Gaudebert gave a cry of amazement.

'Yes, monsieur.' I went on. 'They've got some information, I don't know where from, and they've been looking for the pearls. And certainly not because they intend to give them back, I can promise you that.'

I mopped myself again.

'The Rats' procedure is too unusual for there to be any doubt. And they broke in here hoping to find some more clues.'

I turned to Henriette.

'They knew you were his daughter. Maybe he talked before he lost his mind – enough for them to know they had to concentrate on the Catacombs and the underground passages linked to them, but not enough for them to know exactly where. Anyway, they've been keeping pretty quiet recently. They've probably given up. But we have to concentrate on this area too. And since your father's poems referred to one of the old hiding-places, why not to the present one, too? I've been through them with a toothcomb, and there's one sentence that keeps cropping up regardless of the context, as if he were trying to draw attention to it: *'On the breast or before earthen stars, trout like crossbones weave.'* Now where can you find trout round here? In the lake in the Parc Montsouris? No! Where you *can* find them is in the aquarium in the Reservoir, just a stone's throw away. And the Reservoir is built on a quarry that links up with the Catacombs. I think that's where we've got to look. In the aquarium itself. In the stonework, near where the trout swim to and fro.'

*

Armand Gaudebert phoned me one morning a few days later.

'Permission to visit the reservoir has just come through,' he said. 'It's for this afternoon. Will you come to lunch here first?'

'I don't know—' I began.

'Of course you must,' he said. 'Henriette insists.'

I accepted, and hung up, my heart thumping. Trout before stars! Pearls before swine!

The tiles and frosted glass of the belvedere glinted in the sun. The courtyard of the Reservoir reflected up light and heat, and the gravel burned our feet through the soles of our shoes. It was a beautiful summer afternoon, one of those dream-like days when life seems so good you can hardly believe criminals exist.

The jovial elderly attendant who was to be our guide was a stocky fellow, but the heavy lantern he carried made him lean to one side. He gallantly greeted Henriette first, then looked at Gaudebert, who was standing in the middle of the courtyard looking around as though the place was of particular interest.

'You seem to like it here, monsieur,' he said.

'Yes,' said Gaudebert. 'It's always fascinating to see what these places are like. We're starting with the lower reservoir, aren't we? I believe that's the more interesting one.'

'As you wish, m'sieur,' said the guide. 'It's called the lower one because of its position underneath the other one, but its capacity is far higher. A hundred and twenty-five thousand cubic metres! Just think of that! It'd make a nice swimming pool. It's five metres deep at full capacity – in other words you can't stand in it. But it's not advisable to dive in, either, because it's freezing cold. And now, if you'd care to follow me. This way, lady and gentlemen '

He looked at Henriette, who couldn't have had much on under her blouse and skirt.

'I hope Madame won't be cold,' he said. 'The temperature isn't the same in there as it is out here.'

He was right. After going through a metal door beside some stairs leading up to the belvedere, we found ourselves in a dark and devilishly cold hall. The floor was damp, even muddy in places, and I only just avoided skidding in my crêpe-soled shoes. Gaudebert and his wife took off their sun-glasses.

When our guide opened a second door, we could hear the trickle of running water. He turned on some switches and a series of naked bulbs covered with wire mesh lit up along the walls. While the guide was shutting the door our gaze fell on the trout tanks. The witnesses!

The aquariums are let into the stonework, their walls consisting of the natural rock. There's a constant flow of water running into them, stirring up and polishing and repolishing the multicoloured gravel on the floor. The fish swam swiftly hither and thither behind the thick glass, indifferent to our presence. Under the central aquarium were a number of valves through which clear water fell into a basin that our guide referred to as the drinking fountain. In it were some large test-tubes containing what looked like thermometers.

I gave Gaudebert a nudge and a wink, and pointed at the trout. He started and we exchanged a meaning look. Henriette was watching the gyrations of the fish with a faint smile on her beautiful lips.

We were alone. Our guide had gone off to switch on some spotlights. Gaudebert leant towards me.

'We'll investigate later, eh?'

'Yes, yes,' I whispered.

'But how—'

'Later, as you said.'

'If you'd care to come this way,' said the guide, who'd suddenly reappeared.

Henriette shivered.

'I warned you!' said the old man. 'It's a real ice-house down here.'

'I'm all right,' she said.

'This way, then, please,' he said.

We followed him down a long dark passage with a slippery floor and walls crowding in threateningly on either side. The guide had lit his lantern and its beam, jolting as he walked along, every so often picked out a rivulet or a puddle.

Then suddenly the left-hand wall was replaced by a waist-high parapet. We looked over it, and below us was the reservoir itself, partially illuminated by spotlights.

Countless underground passages stretched out endlessly and identically, their heavy arches reflected in the water, their stone pillars diving out of sight beneath its surface. The great green expanse itself, so deceptively calm, so cold and smooth, looked almost solid. You felt as though you ought to be silent down here; or at most to speak in whispers. The least sound reverberated and died away lugubriously among the distant columns, dark as the frontier of some mysterious ghostly empire.

No matter how firmly you reminded yourself that all this water, once processed and piped, would be used to boil vegetables, make coffee and wash innumerable feet, you couldn't take it in.

Henriette was beside me as we leaned on the parapet and looked silently down into the water. I felt her shiver again, and while I was trying to peer down through the five metres of water to the bottom, she straightened up and moved away. I heard her exchange a few inaudible words with the guide, then came the squelch of his soles on the floor, and a few seconds later another light came on some distance away. I could just make out two figures by it, Henriette's clothes a little patch of white and the guide gesticulating as he answered her questions.

I touched Gaudebert's arm. He started.

'Perhaps we should go and have a look now,' I whispered.

'Yes.' He hesitated. 'But you're not going to do anything foolish, are you?'

'What are you afraid of?' I said. 'That I'll smash the glass of the aquarium and break up the rocks to get at the pearls?'

'Just . . . er, don't do anything foolish, that's all,' he said.

'I won't,' I said.

We moved away from the parapet and began to grope our way back along the slippery corridor through which we'd come. Suddenly Gaudebert let out a muffled exclamation.

'What is it?' I said.

'Nothing,' he said. 'I was feeling my way along the wall and – ' he stopped as if he was short of breath ' – suddenly my hand was suspended in thin air. It was a very peculiar sensation. I wonder whether . . .'

And then suddenly he wasn't there any more. I was left standing on my own in the darkness.

'Where are you?' I growled. 'For God's sake – this isn't the moment to dive in the drink!'

'I'm here,' came a voice which was his, and yet different; further away perhaps. I could still sense he wasn't beside me. I too started to feel my way along the wall. I found an opening, and went through it, almost falling flat on my face in the process. I was sure he must have come this way too, and I was right.

There was a spiral staircase set inside a pillar, and when you'd gone down it for a few steps you came out on a narrow platform right on the edge of the water. Gaudebert was standing there looking out over the reservoir, which from this viewpoint looked even more grandiose and sinister than before. The penetrating damp that rose from the great expanse of water was more noticeable too.

'What are you doing down here?' I said.

'I was looking at those steps,' he said, pressing himself back against the wall so that I could see. 'I was wondering what they were for.'

Another stairway with a metal handrail ran down from the platform and disappeared into the water. It made you think of the submerged city of Ys in the Breton legend.

'They must have to drain the reservoir from time to time,' I said. 'Water's very destructive, and they need to do repairs. They have to get down there somehow, don't they? Look, there's another set of steps over there.'

I'd taken his place at the very end of the narrow platform, and was wondering whether what I was going on about interested him or not. The time had come to act. I prayed to my lucky stars, and to any nymphs who might be around, that I'd have enough warning . . .

Then I was almost caught like a rat in a trap. A dead Montsouris rat floating along in the filthy water of the sewers.

I didn't dodge the blow as effectively as I should have. It glanced off my shoulder. But a shoulder's less fragile than a head, and a blow on the shoulder doesn't make you fall unconscious into a cold and watery shroud. I did lose my balance, though. My foot slipped and my right leg went in up to the knee. Paddling's more amusing at the seaside, and there are pretty girls there as well. I made a hasty recovery and righted myself as best I could, clutching on to the stonework. Then I shot my leg out to get the circulation going again and caught Gaudebert on the shin.

'You've gone too far this time, Judge!' I yelled.

The word 'Judge' ricocheted along the surface of the green water, rebounding from pillar to pillar, and died away in the distance. Perhaps the echoes reached as far as the graveyard where decapitated bodies lie at rest with their heads between their knees.

Then there came a laugh that rolled from arch to arch, setting up another echo. It must have been crystalline once, as sweet and cool as an April morning. But it had become a hideous, almost insane cackle, born of a hatred satisfied at last. Her father might have gone mad as the result of his misfortunes, especially since 1939. But the same tendency must have been inherited by his daughter.

'You hear her, Judge?' I shouted. 'How she's mocking you? She's taken you in completely! Right down to the last pound of flesh!'

The only answer was the all-pervading laughter.

I drew my revolver and climbed cautiously back up to the dark corridor. Every so often I called out a jibe or an insult. But there was no reply. Nothing but the demented laugh of the little girl who'd loved her father and sworn revenge on the man who'd had him sentenced to death. Once she'd found him it was easy enough for her to envelop and then crucify him amid her scented pillows. She might well laugh. First she had ruined him, then she had destroyed him morally. She'd turned him into a criminal, a gangster, one of the wretched fools to whom he in his former pride had never shown any mercy. An excellent joke. But her father, in his hospital room, would never know anything about it. Even if it was explained to him, his disturbed mind wouldn't be able to understand. Which was a pity, in a way.

'Where are you, Judge?' I shouted. 'The game of hide-and-seek's over. What are you trying to do? There's only one place for you when we get out of here. We might as well get it over with!'

No reply. Silence. Even the laughter had stopped. I

walked on a few more steps, and the wall ended and gave way to another parapet. A light nearby shone down on to the water, as calm, as limpid and as cold as nothingness itself. Then I started. Someone was coming towards me along the passage. Before I could tell who it was, a soft seductive voice said:

'Good work, M. Burma. But I'd have preferred it if he'd killed you. He'd never have got away with it.'

She emerged from the clammy darkness and stood in front of me, as white as a spectre. Her blouse was undone at the neck, her bosom rose and fell, her golden-brown eyes glittered strangely. Her red hair seemed to writhe like serpents, her greedy lips to be asking for a kiss.

'He won't get away with it anyhow,' I said. 'And neither will you.'

'Oh, I don't give a damn about myself,' she said coarsely.

'What did you do with the attendant?' I said.

'I socked him one with his lantern,' she said, and smiled. But the smile froze on her face.

From somewhere in the darkness came a metallic creak. I looked quickly towards the place the noise seemed to come from, and saw a brief gleam of light. I hurried forward, the girl close behind me, and found myself facing a heavy steel door. I gave it a push, and to my surprise it opened.

It led into a vast dank-smelling room with two weak light bulbs burning feebly in the lofty ceiling. An iron staircase with non-slip fittings on each step led down to some enormous pipes that disappeared into a tunnel. It was from here that the drinking water set off towards the users' taps. Some of the joints were leaking, and water dripped down with an irritating plopping sound to form small lakes beneath.

I climbed down, clinging to the cold handrail, and followed the giant pipe, studded with huge bolts, into the tunnel.

He'd tried to run away through the sewers, but you have to choose your spot, and the outlet here was too narrow. So he was crouching with his back against the wall, trapped, waiting. Although I was on the alert the violence of his attack took me by surprise. He hurled himself at me and hung on, stifling me with his warm, fetid breath and dragging me to the ground. As we rolled over he hit me again with the pocket cosh he'd used down by the water, and again I avoided the blow as best I could. Then he broke away and made for the stairway with an agility surprising in a man of his age and figure.

When he reached it he began to climb up swiftly. At the top, flattened against the door as if in ambush, was the girl. He went on climbing, but he didn't make it all the way. It was like climbing on ice, and he fell face downward. He got up again with disconcerting speed and grabbed on to the rail. This time he was stopped by a hefty kick from a high-heeled shoe. It landed right in his face, and with a shrill yelp, followed by a bellow like that of a beast in agony, he went down for the second time and lay motionless on his back. One trouser-leg had been pushed back against a step, revealing a hairy calf.

But he didn't stay there long. With a superhuman effort he turned himself over like a pancake so that he was on all fours. Then he raised his head and looked towards me. His face was waxen, puffy and distorted, and the twist at the corner of his mouth looked as if it had been carved with a knife.

'Be upstanding in court!' I taunted. 'Come on! On your feet! Will the accused please rise!'

'Stay where you are,' he said.

He was resting all his weight on his left hand, and in his right was a revolver. My revolver, that he'd pinched from me during our scrap. One really shouldn't get mixed up with public prosecutors!

'Don't be a fool,' I said. 'What can you do, even with the gun? If I'd fallen in I'd have gone straight to the bottom, especially after the meal you gave me – that would have been an accident. But you'll have trouble saying it's an accident if you put a bullet-hole in me. Come on, give me back the gun. I've got a permit, and you haven't.'

I took a step towards him.

'Stay where you are!' he said, and in the eyes beneath those bushy brows there was a hint of madness that stopped me in my tracks.

He grabbed the rail and pulled himself upright.

'Stay there, Burma,' he said. 'Don't try to follow me.'

'Follow you where, you idiot?' I said. 'Even if the pearls were up there in the aquarium you wouldn't have time to find them. But they're not. They never have been. You might say they've never been anywhere. Maybe they never existed.'

'What?' It was more a moan than a question. Now the fun was really going to begin.

'Yes, you red-robed dim-wit,' I went on. 'Castellenot pinched them all right, but he must have got rid of them pretty quickly. He had no choice. You want to know what really happened? It was the Gestapo that got them. The Germans must have been interested in the pearls when they arrested him the first time, and as he wouldn't cooperate they sentenced him to death. Then some other Germans kidnapped him, and *apparently* he escaped. But that was just a lot of eyewash! They *let* him go because he saw the game was up and handed over the loot. The pearls have never been seen since. They must have got lost God knows where during the German retreat. And, you know, the Boches were quite decent to him really: when they nabbed him yet again they spared his life, even though he'd been flirting with the Resistance in the meantime, to refurbish his reputation. Anyway, no pearls.'

'It's not true!' Gaudebert squealed.

'Belt up, Judge!' I said. 'You only say that because someone you thought had reason to know kept telling you the pearls were hidden somewhere, and that with a bit of perseverance you'd find them in the end. But that someone's up there, laughing her head off. Look at her!'

'Say what you like!' he spat out, his grim eyes and the revolver still trained on me. 'Have a good laugh at my expense. I've got nothing left to lose.'

'Just your last illusions,' I said. 'You're going to hear everything. It's only right. Like a condemned man being granted his last wishes.'

I looked up to where Henriette was still standing at the top of the stairway.

'Am I right, Nemesis?'

'Quite right,' she said quietly, evenly.

'Hear that, Judge?' I said. 'She seduced you to avenge her father, and for no other reason. It's not your fault if he's still got a head on his shoulders. Not a very strong one, it's true, but it's there. You didn't take her in and raise her out of some noble sense of atonement, as you like to tell inquisitive private eyes. No, it was *she* who flushed *you* out, what was left of you when the new masters had finished with you, after the Liberation. All very well for you – I wonder what it was like for *her* to sleep with the swine who'd clamoured for her father's head. I wonder whether you didn't get a bit of a sadistic thrill out of it yourself.'

'You bastard,' he said.

'I'm not asking for a confession,' I said. 'She seduces you and gets you caught so fast in her toils that little by little you break with your few remaining friends. And slowly but surely she ruins you. Then, when she's really got you where she wants you, she mentions the pearls just to hasten your downfall, intending to denounce you as soon as you've thoroughly incriminated yourself. I don't know how she manages it, but you both end up at the head of a gang – the Rats of Montsouris, who under cover of burglaries are really looking for a way into the most inaccessible parts of the Catacombs. They're driven on by the belief that they're receiving authentic information via Henriette from her father in the hospital, and that the pearls are hidden down there somewhere. Nemesis must rejoice when she sees you at the head of this band of dolts, getting deeper and deeper into trouble every day, and all for nothing. It'll really be sensational when the scandal breaks.

'But then something even more thrilling happens. While the ex-public prosecutor's lily-white hands are thus occupied, he gets burgled himself. There are two possible explanations. One, it was to draw any possible suspicion away from yourselves. Two, one of the Rats carried out the raid himself in the hope of finding supplementary information and reaching the pearls by himself. Which ever it is, Judge, the rats get into your cheese. And there's a new recruit among them. An old friend of Castellenot's called Ferrand. He noses about and what does he find? Photos of his old mate and of his daughter, and probably letters and documents proving that Castellenot isn't dead but in Sainte-Anne's mental hospital. Ferrand knows the story of the pearls and hopes to be able to get out of his difficulties by finding them. So he goes to see a tough old acquaintance of his, Nestor Burma, with a plan to test him out and discover whether he can trust him enough to tell him the whole story and get his help. But Ferrand must have given away the fact he was in contact with me. Maybe he drew attention to himself by taking too many precautions. Maybe he was overheard phoning me and making an appointment. What can he have to say to a private detective? Quickly, you decide to hatch a counter-plot. You call me and say you want to see me urgently, then you show me a blackmail

tter, supposedly from Ferrand. Now, if Burma mentions
the letter to Ferrand and Ferrand denies having written it,
the detective will give more credence to the word of the ex-
public prosecutor. And if Ferrand tells some slanderous
tale about Gaudebert, Burma will put two and two together
and treat the story with suspicion, as he will even if the
blackmail isn't mentioned at all.'

A curious thing happened at this point in my story.
Gaudebert felt the need to justify himself. All had been lost
for a long time – he knew that better than anyone. But he
began to speak in his own defence. Perhaps it was just a
professional need to argue.

'You're an imbecile, Nestor Burma,' he said. 'Why did
I need to set up such a farce? If I didn't want Ferrand to
talk to you, it would have been quite easy to eliminate him
before he met you.'

I laughed again.

'Objection overruled, as they say in the English courts.
At that time blood hadn't yet been spilled, and you didn't
intend to begin. Perhaps Nemesis suggested it, but you
didn't go along with it. You wanted to wait and see what
Ferrand had to tell me, and hoped you wouldn't have to
go beyond the point of no return. But God had deserted
you, and the Devil was in league with Nemesis. As soon
as I left Ferrand's place he had a visit from another Montsouris Rat, Muhammad, acting on your instructions. He was
meant to check out Ferrand, but took advantage of the
situation to settle an old score, with the result that there
was no more Ferrand.'

She was still standing quietly against the door at the top
of the steps, listening to my story like a good little girl.
Then came that laugh again. The first one was still ringing
in my ears as the second swept like a wave towards the
echoing arches.

'Listen to her, Judge,' I said. 'She couldn't let herself

laugh like that when she found out about Ferrand's death. But she must have wanted to. She's making up for it now.

Now it was Gaudebert's turn to shiver.

'His death was a hell of a blow,' I went on. 'Especially as there was a redhead in the house that night who went and fell right on top of the body, and so became a danger to you herself. The blood had begun to flow from Ferrand's throat, and now there was no stopping it. There aren't any styptic pencils big enough for that kind of thing. Mark you, there's one unsatisfactory aspect about all this from Nemesis's point of view. You've implicated yourself, but not as much as she would like. It wasn't you who killed Ferrand, and it wasn't going to be you who killed Marie Courtenay. One day Henriette would have to force you to commit a crime with your own hand. The chance was bound to present itself one day. And it did.

'I'd found out about the swag, and set off on the hunt as well. But even as I was racking my brains to find the hiding-place (I did come up with probably the only one that ever really existed, but it by now was empty), I turned things over in my mind and it occurred to me that all this might just be a drama of hatred and revenge. So I decided to see if I was right. I contacted you both again and set a trap, telling you the story about the trout and saying I'd got it from Castellenot's sacred texts. Henriette knew the pearls weren't with the trout, but she didn't know I'd made up that part of the poem, so she believed I'd go and visit the reservoir. This was the moment to make Gaudebert commit his crime. She must have told you I was becoming dangerous, and that there'd be plenty of opportunity to get rid of me during this visit. While she took care of the guide, you were to chuck the detective in the drink. The cold drink. And with the copious meal you'd given him heavy on his stomach, he'd be done for. Only I chose this venue precisely because of all the possibilities it offers. You took advantage of them and gave yourself away. When I heard the attendant say: "You seem to like it here", I realized you must have examined the place already, yesterday or the day before, and run through a dress rehearsal in your mind.

'So there we are. The hearing is over as far as I'm concerned. Ladies and gentlemen of the jury, the man before you is accused of—'

'Bastard!' yelled Gaudebert.

I abandoned my flights of oratory and fell flat. I'd thought that as he hadn't opened fire at the beginning of my speech, he wouldn't fire at all. But he was a typical lawyer. No hope of reading his thoughts or anticipating his reactions. I was surprised I'd even got him to rub me out. Sheer luck, no doubt. The revolver was spitting bullets, but none of them ricocheted off the pipe I'd sheltered behind. I took a chance and lifted my head.

He was standing with his back to me, half-way up the metal staircase. His right arm hung limply at his side, still clutching my gun. A few steps above him Henriette was clinging to the railing and swaying backwards and forwards in a way that brought my heart into my mouth. He must have emptied the entire magazine into her stomach.

I leapt from my hiding place, and he turned in my direction. Then, as though activated by a spring, he climbed the remaining steps, grabbed the girl in both arms and hurled her back down the stairs. I saw her come towards me, her limbs sprawling like those of a rag doll, her red hair whipped by the rushing air, and her lips drawn back in a grimace from her pretty teeth. And those eyes! They were burning still, their flame fanned by a hatred satisfied at last. She was the daughter of one of society's rats, of a hard case, a gangster. But she was tough and strong-willed. She would struggle against death to savour her revenge. I prayed to whatever God gangsters worship, and to my own can-can girl guardian angel, to let the girl live long enough to produce a statement and get me out of the bloody mess I'd got myself into.

Because there wasn't much hope of catching Gaudebert alive.

He'd slammed the heavy iron door behind him. And after laying the girl down at the foot of the stairs, I went after him. I heard him gallop away along the tunnel, and caught the dry click of a hammer going down on an empty chamber. And then I heard an enormous splash. I stopped, leaned over the parapet and looked down. It was just as I'd thought. Now they'd have to declare the water unfit for human consumption.

I turned slowly back. My foot knocked against a heavy object, and I bent down mechanically to pick it up. I walked towards the entrance. He'd put me on to a really good thing, that dim-wit, Ferrand. 'Worth a few million!'

The sunlight in the courtyard was a like a truncheon blow, and I staggered, half blinded, towards the cops who'd arrived just in time to nab me. The watchman must have come to and sent for them. Dimly I saw their guns trained on me as I walked forward, and I raised my hands as high as I could above my head, throwing a huge shadow across the burning hot gravel. The heavy object I'd picked up was still in my right hand. My revolver.

Ferrand had put me on to a really good thing. All I'd got out of it was trouble. And now the cops were getting ready to give me more.

Paris, 1955

Léo Malet
**120 rue de la Gare** £3.99

*'We'd arrived in Lyon, Lyon-Perrache station to be precise. It was two o'clock by my watch and I had a nasty taste in my mouth . . .'*

Nestor Burma has seen a lot of strange men die in his time. So when a soldier without a name utters the dying words '120 rue de la Gare', the chief of the famous Fiat Lux Detective Agency is only mildly intrigued.

It's when a colleague meets death gasping the same phrase that Burma's interest – and fury – are fully aroused. Time to take out his pipe, discover the secret of the morbid address and nail the murderer in one fell swoop.

*One problem. Where is 120 rue de la Gare?*

All Pan books are available at your local bookshop or newsagent, or can be ordered direct from the publisher. Indicate the number of copies required and fill in the form below.

Send to: **CS Department, Pan Books Ltd., P.O. Box 40, Basingstoke, Hants. RG21 2YT.**

or phone: 0256 469551 (Ansaphone), quoting title, author and Credit Card number.

Please enclose a remittance* to the value of the cover price plus: 60p for the first book plus 30p per copy for each additional book ordered to a maximum charge of £2.40 to cover postage and packing.

*Payment may be made in sterling by UK personal cheque, postal order, sterling draft or international money order, made payable to Pan Books Ltd.

Alternatively by Barclaycard/Access:

Card No. 

Signature:

Applicable only in the UK and Republic of Ireland.

*While every effort is made to keep prices low, it is sometimes necessary to increase prices at short notice. Pan Books reserve the right to show on covers and charge new retail prices which may differ from those advertised in the text or elsewhere.*

NAME AND ADDRESS IN BLOCK LETTERS PLEASE:

....................................................................................................................................

Name ———————————————————————————————

Address ———————————————————————————————

————————————————————————————————————

————————————————————————————————————

————————————————————————————————————

3/87